A PEEP AT "NUMBER FIVE"

"I've been to pay my tax-bill, and it was **twenty dollars less than**
I expected." — Page 274.

A PEEP AT "NUMBER FIVE"

OR

A CHAPTER IN THE LIFE OF A CITY PASTOR

By

MRS. ELIZABETH (STUART) PHELPS

(H. Trusta, pseud.)

American Fiction Reprint Series

BOOKS FOR LIBRARIES PRESS

FREEPORT, NEW YORK

1971

First published in 1852
(Item #1885; Wright's AMERICAN FICTION 1851-1875)

Reprinted 1971 in *American Fiction Reprint Series*

PS 2557
P4

INTERNATIONAL STANDARD BOOK NUMBER:
0-8369-7050-0

LIBRARY OF CONGRESS CATALOG CARD NUMBER:
70-164573

PRINTED IN THE UNITED STATES OF AMERICA

A PEEP AT "NUMBER FIVE;"

OR,

A CHAPTER IN THE LIFE OF A CITY PASTOR.

BY

H. TRUSTA,

AUTHOR OF "THE SUNNY SIDE," "KITTY BROWN," ETC.

EIGHTH THOUSAND.

BOSTON:
PHILLIPS, SAMPSON, AND COMPANY.
1852.

ANDOVER: JOHN D. FLAGG,
Stereotyper and Printer.

CONTENTS.

1*

A PEEP AT "NUMBER FIVE."

CHAPTER I.

THE PARTY.

THE moon was up, shining with a cold, beautiful light upon a wintry spot. No one was stirring there, and had not the wind moaned and groaned through the huge tree-tops, the silence would have been quite unbroken. This desertion of the streets at so early an hour, was an unusual circumstance; the reason of it was, that most of the people who lived in this bleak spot were preparing for an evening party.

On a little elevation there stood a brick building with which the moon was coquetting. Now she chased over it huge fantastic shadows; now she silvered its old bricks, and now smiles vanished, and frowningly she looked upon it as it stood, dark and dreary, under the moaning elms. This building was a Theological Seminary, and lights, twinkling here and there in its windows, intimated that

probably there was more cheer within than without. This was true, at least of one room, — the corner room, third story, front, where Mr. Holbrook
sat by his little stove with his feet elevated, his
chair tipped back, and a book in his hand, taking
a student's comfort. This was disturbed by the
remark of his chum : "That it was high time they
were getting ready." With a sigh the book was
put down.

"I have no taste for evening parties, John," said
he, "I wish I need not go."

"Neither have I," replied his chum. "The fact
is, we go too little into society; it is quite an undertaking for us. What we are to do by and by
when we are fairly out in the world, I do not
know. If we should chance to settle in a city, we
should be like a fish out of water."

"No danger of my settling in a city," said
young Holbrook, "so *that* argument fails; but if
I must go, I must I suppose, but I declare, I'd
rather preach for the President next Sabbath."

"It wouldn't kill you to do both," said Mr. John.

Holbrook laughed. "At any rate, I shall not
offer my services," said he ; "how is it out,— cold?"

"Cold enough, and the moon seems to be in a
cloud just now, but I think we shall have a clear
evening."

"I wonder who is to be there," said Mr. Holbrook.

"That is no matter, so far as you are concerned, if Miss Lucy is one of them."

"You are a famous man for taking things for granted," said Mr. Holbrook, smiling, but preparing to make his evening toilette. He was soon dressed, but if the truth must be told, not well dressed. His rusty coat hung loosely and awkwardly about his fine figure, and his linen was coarse and ragged on the edges, for he was poor, and was struggling through his theological course with close economy. Some aid he received from the Education Society, but this was insufficient to meet all his wants, as his wardrobe plainly showed. Yet, poor as his dress was, it could not conceal a certain nobleness of carriage, which, after all, made him appear as well as some students who, comparatively, were "clothed in purple and fine linen."

By the time Mr. Holbrook and his friend went out, the wintry spot, of which we have spoken, was alive with people. The professors and their families, the students, the near and distant neighbors, were moving in the same direction. Some were riding, and merry sleigh-bells chimed a chorus to merrier voices. The moon, growing good-natured, condescended to enjoy the scene, and lighted up the road and by-paths as bright as day. The winds, too, ceased their melancholy croaking, and the huge elms, with softened temper, condescended to wave gently their sparkling burden of little stars, and to give graceful motion to the shadows which were delicately crayoned on the pure, unbroken surface of the snow. The keen, cold air, exhilarated those who breathed it, and many a musical laugh came ringing out from under little hoods. Even those who had come reluctantly to the party, found themselves, before they were aware of it, quite in the spirit of the occasion, when, on suddenly turning a corner, they caught sight of the house blazing with light.

"Well, John," said Mr. Holbrook, "I believe I feel better already for coming out."

"I told you so," said Mr. John, "but this is the best part of it; you must remember that we are to play the agreeable for the next three hours."

"Ah me!" replied Mr. Holbrook, "this comes tough on us poor fellows who pore over our books all the week, — this playing the agreeable! What shall we talk about? For my part, I never have any small change when I want it. If they would let us take up 'Decrees,' and discuss it, I should get along bravely."

"You can try it if you wish," said Mr. John, "but I fancy you will find the weather and the moonlight much more to your purpose. You must tell the ladies about the fine sleighing, and wind off with a polite invitation for them to try it with you."

"And pay their own bills?" said Holbrook, laughing, and ringing the bell. The door was instantly opened, and the two friends were ushered into a side room where they found several students in waiting.

"What has brought you out, Holbrook?" said one; "I thought you had a mortal aversion to parties."

"My chum brought me out," said Mr. Holbrook, tossing up his glossy brown hair, and taking a peep at the mirror.

"Of course you do not expect to be believed," said Mr. John. "That is not my concern," was the reply, "but come; I think we shall pass muster; let us go in."

It was amusing to observe the magical effect which the threshold of the drawing-room had upon these young students. Their pleasant gaiety, and easy, natural manner vanished, and with gravity they paid their compliments to the lady of the house in an awkward manner, which did them injustice. Going into a lady's parlor, was to them, going into a strange world, and with an appearance of great resignation to an evil which could not be avoided, they stood for a few minutes near each other, embarrassed, not knowing precisely whom to address.

2

"This is a very cold evening," said Mr. Holbrook, at length, to a lady near him.

"Very cold, sir," was the prompt reply, as if the lady rejoiced to break the silence. Mr. Holbrook dared not raise his eyes to Mr. John, who still stood at his elbow. Not a word was spoken. "Clear and cold to-night," said Mr. John, suddenly addressing another lady. "Yes, sir," was the timid reply.

There is often a fascination about that which we wish to avoid. Mr. Holbrook and Mr. John were exceedingly anxious not to look at each other, and yet, in spite of themselves, their eyes met, and each moved quickly away to hide the smiles which could not be suppressed.

Mr. Holbrook looked about the crowded room, but did not find the face he sought. He was more disappointed than he would have acknowledged, and in consequence became silent. Once or twice a fellow student in passing would give him a friendly knock, which was intended as a hint that he should be more sociable, and he did at length rouse himself and set the ball of chit-chat rolling; but it proved a laborious undertaking, and soon abandoning it, he stole into a corner behind a party, and ventured a sly peep at his watch.

The party who screened him from observation were talking earnestly about the Education Society, and the popularity of its secretary. Some of the ladies were laughing at both, and now and then a student joined them.

"What is your opinion?" said one, turning suddenly so as to bring him into the circle; "you, too, have had some experience in the matter."

This question aroused Mr. Holbrook. He forgot that he was in a party and among strangers. "My opinion is," said he, "that it is a noble enterprise. The churches are indebted to it for many a minister whom they cannot afford to lose, and many a minister owes to it more than he would know how to reckon, — and yet it is often wounded even by those who receive of its bounty. If its machinery, like all others, does sometimes work with too much friction, it is but justice to acknowledge that it does its work well."

"Surely, Holbrook," said one who had joined the ladies' side, and who now stood smoothing down his coat sleeve; "surely, you do not like to go through *this* ordeal?"

"That troubles only those whose character is in their broadcloth," said Mr. Holbrook, with an expressive smile on his lip. In an instant it had vanished, and the poor student stood abashed, finding he had drawn the attention of the company upon himself and the quality of his dress. He sought a retreat, and as he turned, the light from

soft hazel eyes fell upon him, — light full of sympathy and love, — there stood Lucy. Mr. Holbrook immediately joined her with such evident
pleasure, that it made her blush. He would not
again have left her, had not she, in the course of the
evening, delicately reminded him of his duty by
speaking of her own. She left him, to seek other
friends, and he was once more at the mercy of
strangers.

Attempting to make his way through the crowd,
he was at one time blocked in near the gentleman
of the house, and a very beautiful young lady with
whom he was conversing. This was Miss Hubbell, a city-belle. Her figure was large and commanding; her eyes were black, and yet so sparkling, that they seemed like lightning-flashes from
a dark cloud. Her head was finely shaped, and
in her soft raven hair, pearls were tastefully
braided. Ornaments of the same, also, covered
her bare white throat and arms. She was dressed
in crimson velvet, and made a more splendid appearance than any other lady in the room.

To Mr. Holbrook's surprise, he was introduced
to Miss Hubbell. He stood for a moment embarrassed, — he had nothing to say to the proud beauty. She stood perfectly self-possessed, carelessly
playing with her bouquet, and waiting for the profound remark which was apparently on its way.

" This is a fine evening for a social gathering,"
he stammered out at last.

" *Very*," said Miss Hubbell, lifting up her long
eye-lashes, and letting a laughing, flashing glance
fall upon the speaker; she was making merry as
she counted up the score of times in which she
had remarked on the "fineness of the evening."
She was, also, at a glance, taking in the student
from head to foot; ragged collar, rusty coat, and
patched boots! A certain curl in the corner of
her ruby lips, told tales which she did not mean
to have told.

" She thinks," said Mr. Holbrook to himself,
" that I am only a poor ' Theologue,' and not worth
the trouble of entertaining." It was true, she did
think so. He was about turning away to leave
her undisturbed in her opinion, when he again
caught sight of those hazel eyes. This time there
was a peculiar meaning in them, — they seemed
to say, " stand your ground," — at least this was
his interpretation. His half-formed plan of retreat was abandoned; he turned, and once more
looked in the flashing eyes of the haughty beauty,
and this time bore, without wincing, their artillery.
He did, also, what required even more courage ; he
kept his ground bravely against covert smiles of
contempt, and more undisguised expressions of
ennui. In a gentlemanly manner, and yet with

2*

quiet self-respect, which even Miss Hubbell
acknowledged, he re-commenced conversation.
Again was he aroused, and now he displayed
some of that eloquence for which he afterwards
became distinguished. The beauty began to listen. Seizing this advantage, he pressed her
hard; he "sounded the depths of her philoso-
phy," — he entangled her in the subjects on which
her professed knowledge was superficial, — she
was compelled to expose her ignorance. Finding
herself drifting out to sea, she abruptly changed
the conversation. "The poor student, after all,
knows something," thought she, "he has made
me make a fool of myself." Her contempt for
him was converted into respect,— and a little fear
even, mingléd with it. She was glad to retreat,
— and he, with glowing cheeks, came off from the
contest victorious.

The party broke up. The ladies stood in the
hall, closely muffled, but Mr. Holbrook knew
Lucy, and joined her. On their way home, they
talked over the party, and his adventure with Miss
Hubbell. Lucy had observed it with much pleasure. She rejoiced in every occasion which called
out her friend, and gave him more confidence in
himself.

When they reached her boarding-house, (for
she was at the Academy in S.,) she lingered on

the door-step. Evidently, there was something on her mind, of which she wished, and yet was afraid to speak. At length, as she turned the latch of the door, she summoned all her courage, and said, with beating heart: "Mr. Holbrook, I see your collar needs a stitch or two. Will you bring it to me some time?"

"I suppose I *am* shabby," said Mr. Holbrook, in reply, "but I have no one to look after these things."

"If you would let me put in a stitch," said Lucy, stopping short, and leaving the sentence unfinished.

"Well, perhaps I will bring you one."

"Bring all — will you?" said she, in a whisper.

"Why, I have but *four* in the wide world," said Mr. Holbrook, laughing, and bidding her good-night.

CHAPTER II.

THE COLLARS.

It was not very long after the party, before Mr. Holbrook called upon Lucy. Hearing that he was below, she came immediately down to see him, and as she passed through the hall, she noticed that his hat was standing on the table. With light tread she went to it and peeped in. She found, as she hoped, a small roll of collars there, which she quietly slid into her pocket.

Mr. Holbrook made no allusion to them, neither did she, though they at first chatted freely about the party, and the encounter with the city-belle.

Lucy asked, — "What made her manner towards you change so suddenly?" "I do not know," replied Mr. Holbrook, " unless it was that I led her to converse on subjects on which she suspected her own ignorance."

" Perhaps she made the discovery that you knew something," said Lucy. Mr. Holbrook smiled in a way which gratified Lucy. She had observed that at times he was sensitive to his poverty, and awkwardness, and ignorance of the

customs of society, and she felt that he was not
just in his estimate of himself. Lucy had a true
woman's heart, which finds out by instinct the
necessities of the one it loves. Sometimes the
young oak bears the blasts better, for the clinging
of the vine which it supports. Thus the young
man takes a new position among the fair, when
he is known to be a chosen one, — a position
which puts him quite at his ease with them ; and
as to taking a stand among men, that is not beyond his strength.

When Mr. Holbrook first knew Lucy, he spoke
discouragingly of the prospect of his becoming a
preacher. He told her frankly, that in casting
in her lot with his, she had nothing to look
forward to but the very quiet life of a minister's
wife in some retired village. Yet obscure and
humble as was the work which, in his view, was
before him, he often felt unequal to it. It was
with a strange contradiction of feeling that he
thought and spoke of it. Full of enthusiasm, he
was eager to enter upon his life's work, and yet
often was he overwhelmed by a sense of its importance, and borne down by secret self-distrust.
Again, the cloud passed away, and latent powers
stirred within him, and with dim whisperings mur-
mured of some such future success in that great
work, as to startle him, and sometimes cause the

wondering student to bow, humbled and repentant, on account of his pride. Thus he struggled on, as yet ignorant of himself and of the world which was before him.

Lucy, instinctively, sided with those whispering voices. She feared despondency more than ambition for her friend, and she used gentle persuasion to induce him to await in *hope* the decisions of the future. Her cheerfulness had its influence upon him, and gradually he ceased to look forward with so much fear to that time when he should be a preacher of the gospel. He began to speak, not of the very "retired spot," but of some "stirring village," which would now and then peep into his visions. Perhaps he might do good, even there. With Lucy, also, he forgot all about the awkwardness, — the ill-fitting, rusty coat, — the patched boots, — things which occasionally disturbed his equanimity elsewhere. What did she care for those? — she loved him for what he *was*, not for what he appeared to be.

Never had he conversed with her so freely respecting himself and his plans as on this evening. He expressed his deep convictions of the great importance of his work, — and his earnest desire to consecrate himself wholly to it. He spoke of the small parish which he hoped to take, and the advantage it would be to him in giving him time

for study, and this, for some years to come, seemed to him of the utmost importance to his ultimate
usefulness. To Lucy, therefore, any place where
he could be making progress, looked attractive.

Time ran fast while Lucy and Mr. Holbrook
were thus conversing, and it was much later than
usual when he rose to take his leave. She held
the light for him in the entry. As he took up
his hat, he looked in it and smiled, which made
her blush suddenly, for she had, till then, forgotten the collars.

She went up to her room. Her room-mate,
Mary Jay, had retired, and was more than half
asleep. Lucy stepped softly about that she might
not disturb her, and drawing the little stand behind the head of the bed, sat down to make over
the collars.

By and by Mary awoke. "Why, Lucy," said
she, "what are you sitting up all night for?"

"I am sewing," said Lucy; and Mary returned
to her dreams. The next day she excused herself from school; she wished to do some "clear
starching;" and thus the collars were nicely 'done
up,' and Mary Jay was none the wiser for it.
Lucy looked at them with great satisfaction, — for
they were smooth and shining, and who could tell
them from new ones? Gladly would she have
added to this little store, but she had her doubts

whether it would be altogether pleasant to the sensitive feelings of her friend, if she should do so, and her delicacy led her to a right conclusion. He could more easily have done without collars, than to have received them thus, — and who will blame him?

There is a rich and benevolent lady in our city. She likes employment, but has nothing to do. She has an abundance of nice linen on the upper shelf in her closet, but no use for it. It is a stormy afternoon, — no one will call, and she cannot go out. The interesting book is finished, and time is a burden on her hands. Why, now, cannot she get that linen and cut out a dozen collars? She can take those elegant worsteds from the basket on her centre table and make room for the collars, and she can stitch them nicely at her leisure; and her laundress will do them up beautifully; and, if she will but inquire, she can easily find out where are those secret channels through which her bounty will flow in to the "*poor* student," and be received by him most gratefully. Why will not she do it? As she stitches on them, she can sing away for encouragement these words: "Inasmuch as ye did it unto one of the least of these, ye did it unto me."

CHAPTER III.

STRANGERS VISIT THE GREEN MOUNTAINS.

THE theological student's senior year was a short one. Summer, with her long days and glorious nights flew by, and autumn came in with her rich harvesting. On one of her bright days, Mr. Holbrook and his class-mates sung their parting hymn; and with much feeling, bade each other farewell. The occasion was one of deeply solemn interest. It was one of those transition points in the student's career, at which he pauses and looks back thoughtfully over the past, and prayerfully girds on his armor anew, ere he steps forward into the opening arena.

Nearly all the members of this class, had already found occupation; but a few, and among them our friend, Mr. Holbrook, had been less fortunate. His diffidence prevented his seeking places, and may have indirectly prevented their seeking him. At the close of this eventful autumn day, therefore, he found himself a licensed preacher, without a home and without the prospect of a field

3

of labor. A small library, and *six* written sermons comprised his worldly estate; and there seemed to be nothing for him to do, but to retain the "corner room, third story, front," and then trust to Providence for such opportunities to preach as would enable him to earn his daily bread.

Several Sabbaths passed, and he had received no invitation to preach. At length, one of the Professors sent him to supply a vacant church in a very small village, which was perched up on the Green Mountains. This seemed to be just such a place as he had once thought would be his future home; but of late his visions had changed. Untried powers, half awakened, disturbed him with their restless and mysterious calls for a somewhat larger field in which to exercise themselves; it was not, therefore, with entire satisfaction that he looked forward to the prospect of laboring there permanently. But no other door opened for him; and he felt that there was great significance in the command: "Whatsoever thy hand findeth to do — do." He accordingly was soon preaching as a candidate to the villagers in the Green Mountains.

On the second Sabbath that he spent there, he observed, sitting in one of the front pews of the church, a gentleman who was apparently a stranger, and who seemed to be regarded with respect by the people. After service the minister was introduced to Mr. Kennedy. He soon learned, also, that he was from —— city; had the reputation of being wealthy, and, as he paid an annual visit to his aged parents, gave liberally towards the support of the little church of which they had long been members.

On the third Sabbath, Mr. Holbrook was surprised to see Mr. Kennedy in his seat again, and two other gentlemen, also strangers, with him. In the evening, while thinking over the labors of the day, he was waited upon by a committee of the people, who presented a formal request to him, " that he would settle among them." As an inducement, they told him frankly, " Their folks liked him right well; would give him a unanimous call, and would pay him *four hundred dollars a year — and sass*, which, considering their very *peculiar circumstances*, they thought was a pretty good salary for them to offer."

Mr. Holbrook felt that this call, humble as it was, required prayerful consideration; he told them, therefore, he would consider it. Scarcely had this committee left him, when Mr. Kennedy and the two gentlemen entered. They came with a proposition, and it was, that Mr. Holbrook should, on the following Sabbath, go to the city to preach as a candidate in the Downs Street Church. Had the city itself dropped down on the Green Mountains, our young student would scarcely have been more surprised than he was by this proposal. He heard it in silence; indeed, he could not immediately speak. When he did, it was with a voice, which in spite of him betrayed his agitation, that he endeavored to thank them for their expressions of interest in his preaching. " But," said he, " this is so wholly unexpected to me, I cannot talk of it to-night. Give me until to-morrow morning to think of it."

Of course this was acceded to, and after having again expressed a most flattering interest in the preacher and the preaching, the city committee took their leave, promising to call early in the morning.

Sleep was not Mr. Holbrook's business that night, for he paced back and forth in his little room until nearly morning — thinking. It *might be* that he should be called to settle over a city church, a position which presented itself to his young imagination, as a post of command in respect to ministerial influence; he *was* called to settle in an humble nest among the Green Mountains. What now, said those restless voices, which so frequently had disturbed him, by what seemed to him ambitious whisperings? Ah! now, they were timid and silent, and the work for which Mr. Holbrook

thought himself best fitted, was the work of preaching the gospel to the simple mountaineers. A
change came over him in this test-hour, and the
humbler sphere appeared the most alluring. He
shrunk from the more responsible position, — he
felt every way unequal to it, and, had he followed
the bent of his feelings, the call to the larger would
at once have decided him in favor of the smaller
field. But feeling, alone, was not to be followed.
To him, the call to the city appeared one of duty;
it had come in a remarkable manner; he felt that
there was a Providence in it, and he wished to
follow its leadings, suppress his fears, and trust in
God for strength. Many fears were to be suppressed. He had but six sermons, — he wrote
slowly, — he was without experience, — even his
preparatory studies he considered as unfinished,
and had depended upon completing them after he
had settled over some small church. Another
view of the subject also disturbed him. Supposing that he should go, and yet fail of giving satisfaction to the Downs Street people, would not
such a failure, at this period of his career, be a
disadvantage to him? But if duty called, this
anxiety also must be suppressed, — he must do
what seemed to him right, and trust God with the
future.

3*

The struggles of this eventful night resulted in the calm conviction that he must go to the Downs Street Church to preach as their candidate.

It was nearly morning, when he fell into an uneasy slumber, from which he was soon roused by the rumbling of the stage-coach, — Mr. Kennedy came to receive his reply. The invitation to preach at the city church was duly accepted.

Much disappointment at this turn of affairs was felt by the villagers. They had been much pleased with the young preacher, and had fully made up their minds that " he was just the man for them," and they parted from him, sorrowfully.

Mr. Holbrook returned to S., and on arriving there, did not as usual go to his room, but with carpet-bag in hand hastened to Lucy. When alone with her, without waiting even to be seated, he told her what had happened to him, — with a kindling eye, and yet with a blush upon his manly cheek, as if he felt a little fear lest he might seem to be trumpeting his own praises. In subdued tones, and with deep feeling, he expressed his conviction, that " God was leading him, by a way that he knew not," to a turning-point in his life; and that the earnest cry of his heart was, " Let me be still, and follow Thee." As for Lucy, — she stood near him, looking up to his earnest face, — her hazel eyes swimming in tears, and yet beaming with love, — happy indeed she was. But of all this, it is not fair to tell. It was an hour with which a " stranger intermeddleth not."

CHAPTER IV.

THE FIRST SABBATH.

THOSE six sermons which had won simple hearts among the mountains, equally pleased the more refined city people. Mr. Holbrook received a call to the Downs Street Church, and was offered a salary of fourteen hundred dollars a year. This call, after due consideration, he accepted, on condition that six months should be allowed him for preparation, which was granted. Determining to improve this time to the utmost, Mr. Holbrook already saw in imagination a formidable pile of sermons, which should be prepared by the time appointed for his settlement.

This appointed time threw Lucy into great perplexity, for her regular school-course would not be finished until then, and Mr. Holbrook wished to be married as soon as he was ordained.

It is a great affair for a country girl to be married, — there is so much sewing which must be done before she can be considered "ready." One would almost think it was to be Sunday ever after the event, and the shops were to be closed.

Lucy's mother would not think of less than six months' time, and Lucy was therefore obliged either to leave school at once, or to defer her marriage.

To the last proposition Mr. Holbrook would not accede, and to the first he consented reluctantly; so Lucy bade adieu to school and school-girls, and went home, somewhat comforted for her broken course, by a promise from Mr. Holbrook that she should complete it with him.

Mr. Holbrook was so much occupied with sermons and letter writing, that his six months slipped quickly away. He was successful in both these departments, though his sermons occasioned him many hours of despondency. True, having a "people" to write for, he wrote with more care than he once had; but still he found it slow work. Often he felt, that even at that late hour, he must relinquish all idea of settling over a city church. How could he write two sermons a week, such as he should be expected to preach there, when he frequently was obliged to spend three or four days on the half of one? These fears and misgivings found a place in his letters to Lucy. In replying, she once said to him: "Perhaps you will find that you can work three times as fast, when you have three times as much to do. I find it so sometimes. We do not know what necessity will force from us, until it has been tried."

Mr. Holbrook smiled, as he folded her letter. "Who would imagine," thought he, "that Lucy had so wise a head." He returned cheerfully to his tasks ; and the bare walls of that unfurnished corner room, echoed again to profound discussion and eloquent harangue ; for the student preached aloud to them, as he paced back and forth.

The six months were gone. The sermons, a marvellously small pile after all, were carefully packed into a portfolio. The books, from the immovable old blue book-case, were boxed. The clothing which had hung in the closet, was given to a poor fellow who sawed wood about the building, — the student no longer needed it.

In a handsome, well-fitting suit, the work of a city tailor, which added much to the appearance of the outer man, Mr. Holbrook bade farewell to S., and started for the city, which he reached on the day before his ordination. He went at once to the house of his friend, Mr. Kennedy, where he had been cordially invited to remain. He was ordained, and, soon after, took leave of absence for a short time, that he might bring Lucy among his people. They were married, and after a short wedding tour, returned to the city, and again, by special invitation, stopped at Mr. Kennedy's. This afforded Lucy an opportunity of becoming at once personally acquainted with Mrs. Kennedy,

which she found a great advantage to her. Her
first appearance among the Downs Street people,
she has herself described in a letter to her old
room-mate, Mary Jay, from which letter the following extracts are selected.

"MY DEAR MARY:— It was early on Saturday
morning when we arrived in this great city. They
say the "honey-moon" lasts but four weeks; if this
is the case, ours was then half over. Our journey
was a delightful one. We scarcely saw a cloud
until Friday afternoon, and were quite unprepared
to find it raining on Saturday like a flood. It was
so early when we came up from the boat, that I
was hardly awake, and my dulness and the rain
combined, gave me my first fit of home-sickness.
We drove slowly up a long street, and I looked
from the carriage window, trying to read the door
plates through the mist. Pretty soon I read the
name — Kennedy, and here our carriage stopped.
I did not move, but looked at Charles and tried to
smile, as I faltered out: 'This is not home.' 'No,'
he said, 'but you shall go home next week if you
would like to.' This promise cheered me; so I
summoned all my resolution, and entered the
house as if I were pleased to get there. Mrs.
Kennedy met me as kindly as if I had been her
own daughter; she kissed me, and then turned to

give her minister a hearty welcome. I felt for a
moment that I had reached home. Pretty soon
Mr. Kennedy insisted upon it, that we should go
to our rooms and rest until breakfast. We found
our room in beautiful order. Vases of fresh flowers were standing here and there; a white satin
toilette cushion, elegantly painted, ornamented the
dressing-table, and everything wore an air, not
only of beauty, but of comfort. We both felt its
pleasant influence, and Charles seemed so glad
to return to his people that I began to be glad too,
and no longer wished myself back at school. I
do like though, to recall old school-times. By the
way, did you ever find out that I sat up one night
to make over collars for a certain student of my
acquaintance? I'll tell you all about it when we
meet, and we can have a laugh over it now.

"Well, at length we were called down to breakfast. Mrs. Kennedy met us at the foot of the
stairs, and invited us to step into the parlor
a minute. On the centre-table stood a basket
of fine grapes. I took up a card which was
lying on them, and found this on it, ' For Mrs.
Holbrook, with Mrs. Gay's love.' Was n't it a
pleasant attention? ' If your people pet me because I am the minister's wife,' said I to Charles,
'I am afraid they will spoil me ; I am not used
to it.' Mrs. Kennedy was standing near me, and

she laughed heartily at this remark. 'I do not know,' said she, 'about their spoiling you, but I sometimes tell them they must not spoil him, — for they do make so much of him.'

"But there is no use in trying to tell you all which has happened, I have not time; I must skip all the rest that comes before the first Sabbath.

"Now this first Sabbath had been a great bug-bear to me. I had thought of it with a beating heart. I knew it would prove a trying ordeal. To begin with, I was puzzled how to dress. I supposed I ought to wear something a little *bridish*, and yet I did not wish to dress on the Sabbath, in any such way as would attract attention. I wanted to ask Mrs. Kennedy's advice, but did not exactly like to do it; so I did as well as I knew how.

" The rain had ceased the night before, and we had a clear sky, though a cool day. While we were walking to church, I wondered if the sun shone on any happier hearts than ours, — we were together and alone. Mr. and Mrs. Kennedy had slipped around by another way, designedly, I have no doubt. When we reached the church, Charles stepped forward, opened the door, and then walked so briskly up the aisle, I could scarcely keep pace with him. I had, at a glance, a view of a large, pleasant, well filled church, and

4

also noticed a stirring and turning of many
heads. All this time, I was very conscious that
I was making my entreé 'on a hand gallop,' and
this, added to the novelty of my situation, struck
my ludicrous vein. I need n't tell you, Mary,
my infirmity about laughing. What would n't I
have given not to have laughed then; but I did,
and I could not help it. I was glad, I can assure
you, when we reached the pastor's pew. This
pew, or slip rather, as they say here, is a fine one.
It is cushioned, carpeted, and furnished, and there
am I to sit alone. I got into the corner, and took
up a nice white fan, which was lying there, to
play with, for I scarcely knew where to look.
By and by, I ventured a peep at the pulpit, for I
did n't care if the pulpit did look at me. All I
could see was a little line of brown curls, just
above the big Bible. My heart was beating fast,
though I was trying to keep calm, and it was some
time before I was able to look about me. When
I did so, I observed that the gentlemen were
sedate, and apparently devotional; but the ladies'
bonnets were still in commotion, and now and then
I caught a glimpse of bright eyes peeping from
under them. I knew they were all looking at
poor little me, and it almost made me laugh again.
What do you think, Mary; shall I ever be *sober*
enough for a minister's wife? You do n't know

how much I wished, that day, that you were with me.

"After a voluntary, we rose for prayer, and through this, and the sermon which followed, I think the minister had all the attention. After the benediction was pronounced, I remained quietly standing in the corner. The ladies lingered as they passed, evidently wishing to catch a glimpse of me; and I made an effort to raise my eyes and appear at my ease. A vain effort, I imagine, for they soon passed quickly by, as if they understood the reason of my embarrassment; a courtesy for which I sincerely thanked them.

"Callers — callers, — I must run. Good-bye. Will write more next time. Let me hear soon, and believe me as ever,

Yours,   Lucy."

CHAPTER V.

TAKING A HOUSE.

Mr. and Mrs. Holbrook were anxious not to remain too long in their pleasant quarters at Mr. Kennedy's; but from one cause and another, their visit extended over several weeks. Then they made up their minds to commence housekeeping. Lucy's father had given her a few hundred dollars, her marriage dowry, and this, with what the people were ready to advance of Mr. Holbrook's salary, seemed to them abundantly sufficient to furnish a house, for their habits and taste were simple, and their wants few.

This plan being decided upon, both the young minister and his wife were anxious to carry it into effect; and the more they thought and spoke of it, the more fascinating became the idea of having a house of their own; and they were in a hurry to choose the object upon which to bestow their interest. The morning papers were carefully searched, and the little words "To Let," never failed of attracting attention. Afternoons were devoted to long walks from one distant street to another, — to travelling over houses, getting and returning keys, and yet no progress was made towards a selection. There was some difficulty with all. This one was rented too high ; that one was too far from the church; the other one contained no suitable room for a study.

"Well," said Mr. Kennedy to Mr. Holbrook, one day at dinner, "have you found a house yet?"

"That is a question I cannot answer," said Mr. Holbrook, laughing. "House-hunting is not precisely what I thought it was ; it is not easy to suit ourselves, I find. Still, we have fixed upon two, either of which will do. Can you go with us to look at them before we decide?"

"Certainly, with pleasure," said Mr. Kennedy.

"So will I," said Mrs. Kennedy, "we are all interested in our minister's house."

Immediately after dinner, they all went out on this business. Passing up a narrow and rather dark court, they first entered a small, new brick house. Here they found a hall, small and irregular, a china-closet having been taken out of it. On the lower floor was one parlor of moderate size, and back of this a little room containing two windows, which, Lucy remarked, "seemed to have been made for a study;" a small dining-room and kitchen below, which were damp, and numerous small chambers, comprised the remain-

4*

ing accommodations. Mr. and Mrs. Kennedy examined one room after another in silence. At length Mr. Kennedy inquired, " What strikes you as being particularly desirable in this house, Mr. Holbrook ? "

" I hardly remember," said he, " we have looked at so many ; what was it, Lucy ? O, yes," continued he, laughing, " the paper and the little study took Mrs. Holbrook's fancy."

Lucy admitted this.

" I suppose," said Mr. Holbrook, " as we have been brought up in country farm-houses, we are ready to think any of your modern improvements in building very wonderful."

" Perhaps we had better go now and look at the other one you have thought of," said Mr. Kennedy.

" You will not find that at all *modern*," remarked Mr. Holbrook. In order to reach it, they left the narrow court, and entered a wide street. Quite at the head of it was another little court down which they turned, and stopped, at length, before a wooden house which had a small side yard. Mr. and Mrs. Kennedy looked at one another and smiled, and Mr. Holbrook observed it.

" I am afraid you will not like this as well as you did the other," said he, opening the door.

" Let us see what it is," said Mrs. Kennedy;

entering the parlor. "What a funny old-fashioned room, — see! one, two — four small windows, and do look at those cupboards built in the corners! That is odd, — I guess some old maid lived and died here. What comes next?"

"The kitchen," said Lucy, "and a snug little room for a study beyond it." "I never!" said Mrs. Kennedy, looking in, "that was used as a pantry when they pastured the cows in the street, I know."

"It is quite as large as Pres. Edwards's study was," persisted Lucy. "Yes, well, let us look up stairs," said Mrs. Kennedy, — "take off your hats," said she to the gentlemen, "you cannot enter with them on."

"The ceiling is *very* low," remarked Mr. Kennedy, "and what, sir, particularly pleased you in this house?"

"The attraction here," said Mr. Holbrook, "was that bit of a yard, with the elm-tree. Mrs. Holbrook was very willing to give up some comforts within doors, for the sake of green without."

"This is not a suitable house for you," said Mrs. Kennedy, "it will not answer at all."

"We are just where we started, then, said Mr. Holbrook. "I wish," said Mrs. Kennedy, "you would trust Mr. Kennedy and me with this business. It seems a pity to have it take up any

more of your time.   Our people are beginning to
call now, too, and they are disappointed to find
you 'not at home.'"

"I must go about my work," said Mr. Holbrook,
seriously.   "Yes, you can," continued Mrs. Kennedy, "you are not to be disturbed mornings.   I
have taken care of that.   I told the people they
must keep away in the morning, for if they came
I should not call you down.   For my part, said I,
I am not willing to lose my Sabbaths, and if our
minister will take charge of our Sabbaths, we
must take charge of his study-hours."

"I thank you for this," said Mr. Holbrook,
warmly; and he resolved that he would return to
his duties, and leave the house-hunting, with all
its interests, in the hands of his friends.

After this, for some time, Mrs. Kennedy was
out a great deal, and Mr. Kennedy appeared full
of business.   The minister and his wife were
obliged to await results, patiently, and were at
length rewarded by hearing that two houses had
been found, pleasant, convenient, and suitable, and
they had only to make a choice between them.
They went to see them, and found them to be as
had been described.

"On the whole, I prefer this one," said Mr.
Holbrook, "what do you say, Lucy?"

"I prefer this, — but — "

"But — what?"

"The paper is so soiled and ugly."

"You always look at the paper the first thing," said Mr. Holbrook, laughing. "Why should n't I?" said Lucy, "you know we have no pictures to decorate our walls, and the style of the paper can be made to add much to the cheerfulness of a room."

"That is a mere trifle," said Mr. Kennedy, "the house is to be repainted and papered throughout, and Mrs. Holbrook can have her own choice. Indeed, we can stop at a paper store on our way home, if you have time."

Lucy was delighted by this proposal, and when they entered the shop, and many rolls were opened before her, — her heart seemed to be in her eyes, so interested was she. Her first choice was for the study. She was intent on making the study the pleasantest room in the house. Her selections were made with good taste, but with an utter forgetfulness of *price.*

Mr. Holbrook was the first to think of it. "I do not know," said he to Mr. Kennedy, "but that we have selected too expensive paper."

Mr. Kennedy exchanged glances with his wife. "No, sir, no difficulty on that point; take just what pleases you."

This was done to Lucy's entire satisfaction, —

and the house, "*Number Five*," was rented for the Rev. Charles Holbrook.

Since many repairs were to be made before possession was given, Mr. Holbrook proposed removing to a boarding-house; but to this proposition his hospitable friends would not listen. They kindly insisted upon his remaining with them until his own home should be ready.

CHAPTER VI.

WHILE "Number Five" was repairing, Lucy
wrote a few letters. As the one to Mary Jay took
up her new experience where the last one had left
it, a few extracts may not be uninteresting here,
and may serve to occupy the time while we wait
for the painters.

" DEAR MARY: —

    *   *   *   *   *   *   *

— and this brings me to the first church meeting which I attended as a minister's wife. It is a
long walk you know from Mr. Kennedy's to our
vestry, at least I call it so ; and that evening
it seemed to me the dim and narrow streets
through which we passed were interminable. I
do not know why Charles took me through them,
unless it was to make the walk still longer. I
was glad when we emerged into familiar places.
All at once it came over me like news, that here
was poor little I going with the minister, for the
first time on a week day, to show myself to his

people as his wife. I could not help recalling
those times when you and I used to go out of an
evening together. What a tremor I was in sometimes; how half glad and half frightened I used
to be when the meeting was over, — do you remember? Ah! those were days of half-fledged
hopes, — fluttering and not daring to take wing.
'Now,' thought I, 'much that I dreamed about
has proved true;' and the two parts of my short
history came together in such a way as set me to
thinking, and soon caused a re-action of spirits —
from being thoughtful, I became gleeful. But what
do you imagine my sympathizing companion did?
Why, wrap his cloak about his mouth, — pull his
hat down, and bid me 'hush,' for he was getting
ready to speak. Alas! I could remember when
it was the gentleman's business to entertain the
lady he attended, but times are changed; and now
I have a new lesson to learn, to be *sober* and
behave with propriety on all occasions — for I am
a minister's wife! I did try then, for full five
minutes, but all in vain. The robin in the spring
has not a heart more full of song than I had, and
as I could not sing in city streets, there was no
resource for me but a frolic. I had one all to
myself — for *he*, you know, was about better business. Pretty soon we came in sight of the vestry,
and I was at once sobered. I began to realize

where we were going, which, in the gush of feeling, I had almost forgotten.

"We entered the hall, and the minister seated
me somewhere near the centre of it. The ladies,
who were in the slip, politely moved to give me
room, and I sat down, in the midst of our people,
as fresh in spirit as a child on a June morning.
I very soon became much interested in the exercises. I was particularly struck with the *heart*
that appeared in them. The singing I enjoyed,
and the plain remarks which plain church members made, for they were made with much sociality and apparent sincerity. The crowded room,
the attentive faces, the earnest cheerfulness of the
place, took hold of my feelings. Our people seemed to have come away gladly from the busy world,
to sit together, and talk and sing of that ' better
land.' I forgot that I was a stranger among them,
and they forgot it; for the time, I was as one
of them, and I felt that it was good to be in that
company of Christ's chosen ones. But, after the
benediction was pronounced, this aspect of affairs
changed. I was no longer one of them, I was
the minister's wife. Every head seemed turned
towards me, and I found myself in the midst of a
sea of eyes. Right — left — before — behind, —
eyes, eyes, eyes. Never before had I such a keen
sense of the fact, that God has provided us with

a double share of these conveniences.   In the gray-
ish light of the vestry, the effect of so many eyes
was exceedingly curious.   Here was a sweet face,
and at half a glance I had its mild hazel eye ; and
there, in the corner, a pair of coal black ones were
looking me through.   I turned away, and the light
from two soft blues smiled upon me.   I smiled in
return, and then caught an odd twain looking, one
at me, and one at the minister.   All this passed
quickly.   I said to myself, ' bear it bravely a few
minutes, and the worst will be over ;' but the minutes seemed to lengthen, and the people were in
no haste to move.   As it was not Sunday, they
were determined to have a good sight at me.
When Charles joined me, we were obliged to
make our way out slowly ; but when we did reach
the door, I can tell you, I cleared the steps at a
bound.   How glad I was to be through with it.
So, dear Mary, you see I have been exhibited as
a minister's wife, and have survived ; — that, to
comfort you.

    " We are going to house-keeping, — have taken
' Number Five.'   Come and make us a visit as
soon as you can.

Affectionately, yours,

LUCY H."

CHAPTER VII.

"NUMBER FIVE" IN ORDER.

WHILE the pastor's house was undergoing repairs, Mr. and Mrs. Kennedy were out most of the time. Lucy wished to buy her furniture, but she could do nothing without Mrs. Kennedy, and whenever she mentioned it, Mrs. Kennedy immediately advised deferring it until the house was done; and, in addition to this, seemed very anxious that Mr. and Mrs. Holbrook should not go to "Number Five" until the landlord sent the keys.

"There is so much in first impressions," said she, "I do not want to have you go there until the litter is cleared away." She was so urgent about it, they consented not to go until she should give them leave.

Yet Lucy was impatient to select her furniture, and was therefore very glad when Mrs. Kennedy said to her one morning after breakfast, —

"Now, Mrs. Holbrook, this is a beautiful day, and I think your house will soon be done, and if you please, I will go with you to the carpet-stores.

You can choose what you like, and Mr. Holbrook can drop in, in the afternoon, and look at them."

Lucy was not long in getting ready, and they went out at once. She soon found how necessary it was to her to have Mrs. Kennedy with her, for had she been alone, she could not have told what did please her. One's mind gets into a tangle in a carpet-store. Opinions and wishes run into one another like the different patterns and colors of the carpets. Here is this in these colors, how very pretty; and there it is again in those colors, and who can tell which is the prettier?

Poor Lucy sat down on a roll quite in despair. "You like this?" said Mrs. Kennedy.

"Yes, very much, and that too, and I do not know which is the prettiest. What do you think?"

"Roll away those," said Mrs. Kennedy to the boy, "and then we can tell better."

With Mrs. Kennedy's assistance, and the final sanction of the minister, the carpets were chosen, and were to be left in the store until called for. All this was done, and yet Mrs. Kennedy was away from home more than ever.

One morning she made her appearance, looking much pleased. "There!" said she, "I think they will finish at "Number Five" to-day, and to-morrow morning I shall run down and have it

cleared up, and then in the afternoon we will all
go together and see it."

On the morrow, Mrs. Kennedy went out immediately after breakfast, and was seen no more until dinner was on the table. " O, I am late," said
she, " well, never mind. The paint is dry, and
everything is ready. We will hurry our dinner,
so as to get off before any one calls."

" Why, you are in haste, wife," said Mr. Kennedy, as she rang for the dessert before the meat
was carved ; " which shall we eat first ? "

" No matter, — both together, to-day ; I promised we would be there in half an hour."

What did ail Mrs. Kennedy ? She was much
excited ; had a fortune been left her ? Lucy, also,
became excited, without knowing why, — no one
was disposed to " tarry at the wine," so they were
soon on their way to "Number Five."

As they were going up the steps of the house,
Mr. Kennedy handed the key to Mr. Holbrook,
with a smile, and he, taking it, went in, with Lucy
close behind him. Lo ! there was " Number Five,"
beautifully furnished. The chosen carpets had
been made and put down ; the furniture which had
been admired was all there, and the choice paper
decorated the walls. A door, partly open, re-
vealed a well filled china-closet. A bright fire
burned in the parlor grate, and another in the

5*

convenient cooking-stove, and in the dining-room
stood the tea-table, neatly spread. Passing on,
hurriedly, up stairs, the party entered the study.
They found it pleasantly furnished, and the adjoining chamber, also, supplied with all things
needful.

Mr. Holbrook and Lucy stood still, silent with
astonishment. Tears were in their eyes, but not
a word did they speak. Mrs. Kennedy was
laughing at herself, because "she was such a fool
as to cry," and Mr. Kennedy, after stammering
some half intelligible sentences, walked away to
the window. Thus had the Downs Street people
given their young pastor a home ; and very gratifying would it have been to them, could they just
then have taken "a peep at Number Five," and
seen the deep feeling with which their kindness
was received.

"You will spoil us," said Lucy, turning to Mrs.
Kennedy. The minister's heart was still too full
for words, — so he walked quickly back to his
study, and entered it alone. He looked about
him ; the carpet, window-shades, and table cover,
had been selected by an occulist, and selected
with special reference to the comfort of a student.
They were of that peculiar cheerful green which
refreshes the eyes and the spirits, like the green
of summer, and the paper, Lucy's choice, har-

monized with them. Mr. Holbrook walked to
the window to view the prospect. In the distance
was the bay, and nearer, the old church tower;
and yonder, through the opening, might be seen
glimpses of sunset clouds. He stood a moment
lost in thought, and then returning to his study-
table, he sat down and leaned his head upon his
hands. The cheerful study, and the pleasant
prospect no longer filled his mind, for they had
led him to think of the great work to which he,
in God's providence, had been called. So important did it now appear to him, and so dear seemed
the interests of his people, that he most fervently
and solemnly dedicated this room to their service.
Here would he labor and pray for them; here
should be the little Eden, into which the tempta-
tion of trifling pursuits should never enter. In
remembering the wants of his people, Mr. Holbrook forgot his own.

"Charles, Charles," said Lucy, calling him from
the foot of the stairs, "a carriage has stopped at
our door, — will you come down?"

"*Our door*," thought he, as he obeyed the summons, "this is the first time we have ever said
that."

Mr. Kennedy had answered the bell, and was
waiting upon a lady into the parlor. She introduced herself to Lucy, as Mrs. Talbot.

"Your mother," said she to her, "was an old friend of mine, and I wished to become acquainted with her daughter; so I have called as soon as I heard of your being here."

There was something in Mrs. Talbot's words and manner which immediately put Lucy at her ease, and she introduced her husband and friends without embarrassment.

Mrs. Kennedy knew Mrs. Talbot well by sight, though she had never before spoken to her. Indeed, she was well known in the city, as the widow of a wealthy and distinguished citizen. Mrs. Kennedy was evidently pleased that it was Mrs. Talbot, who made the first call upon their minister's wife in her new home; and that Mrs. Holbrook received her so prettily.

"Have you been long at house-keeping?" inquired Mrs. Talbot of Lucy.

"About an hour, I believe," said Lucy, laughing. Then what did she do, but just tell Mrs. Talbot the whole story. How Mr. and Mrs. Kennedy had managed to keep them away from "Number Five," and succeeded so well, that they had never mistrusted what was going on; how the people had furnished the house, and done it liberally, in good taste; and Lucy, in telling the story, became animated and eloquent, and Mr. and Mrs. Kennedy sat still, listening, and enjoyed it to their hearts' content.

"I should like to show you my study," said Mr. Holbrook.

"I should like to see it," said Mrs. Talbot, rising and following him, as with evident pleasure he led the way up stairs. He opened the door, and then looked round with a countenance so expressive and beaming, as to call forth intelligent glances between Mr. and Mrs. Kennedy.

"This," said he to Mrs. Talbot, "this is my beau ideal of a study."

Mrs. Talbot praised it, and it certainly merited praise; and if she was not as enthusiastic in her admiration as the young pastor was, it must be remembered that she had never seen that old "corner room, third story, front," with which he was constantly comparing it.

When the study had been thoroughly discussed, Lucy opened the door into the adjoining room. "And this, too, they furnished," said she, "and the kitchen, — that is very complete; why, they have even put up a clock."

"A clock is very necessary in a minister's kitchen," said Mrs. Talbot, "for his minutes are precious. But my dear Mrs. Holbrook, I do not see but that you must have a house-warming."

"A house-warming?" said Lucy, "what do you mean?"

"You must throw your house open, and invite all your people to come and see you."

"I should like to do that very much," said Mr. Holbrook, "it would afford me such an opportunity as I wish, to thank them."

"Such occurrences are not uncommon among you, I think," said Mrs. Talbot to Mrs. Kennedy.

"O no," was the reply, "they are frequently done.

"Then why cannot we have a house-warming?" said Lucy. "You can, if it would be agreeable," said Mr. Kennedy, smiling.

"Then we will consider that settled," said the minister.

"And a very suitable way it will be of acknowledging the kindness of your people," said Mrs. Talbot.

After some further conversation on the subject, Mrs. Talbot rose to leave. She gave a hand to the minister and his wife, and said to them, kindly, "We must be friends; come and see me soon, and let me know of all which interests you. If you have a house-warming, Mr. Holbrook, remember that I must have a finger in the pie."

Lucy stood at the window looking after her, as she drove away. "It is very pleasant," said she, "to meet any one who knows my mother. I feel as if Mrs. Talbot were an old friend."

"She is a very fine lady," remarked Mr. Kennedy; "distinguished for her active benevolence."

"Yes," said Mrs. Kennedy, "I have always liked her. She has a great deal of good sense, and then her manners are, I think, a model for a lady. There is nothing ceremonious, formal, or artificial about her; and in regard to all the proprieties of life, her judgment is excellent. Since she has suggested the house-warming, I have been thinking our people would be much pleased with it."

While they were talking, the afternoon slipped away, and night fell on them, like a gray mantle.

"We *must* go home," said Mrs. Kennedy, rising suddenly. "It is getting dark."

"We *are* at home," said Mr. Holbrook, "will not you spend the night with us?"

"No, I thank you," said Mrs. Kennedy, laughing heartily.

Still the minister and his wife lingered as if reluctant to leave their new quarters.

"You wish to stay, do you not?" said Mrs. Kennedy; "well, your fires are burning nicely, and there is an abundance here to eat, and I will send Jane in to help you, so you shall stay if you wish."

Gladly did Mr. and Mrs. Holbrook accede to this. They wished to sit down with each other, for the first time, alone in their own home. They had much to say about the present, and many plans to make for the future.

CHAPTER VIII.

THE HOUSE-WARMING.

THE Downs Street people had furnished " Number Five" thoroughly, as far as they had furnished it at all; but many things were necessarily left for Lucy to add. She wished to complete it before the house-warming, but soon found she could not shop without Mrs. Kennedy. To her surprise, Mrs. Kennedy was not as ready to go out with her as she had once been. Lucy said to her, " I am afraid I tax you by coming so often, but the truth is, I do not know how to buy without you."

" Not at all," said Mrs. Kennedy, " I like to go ; but since I now no longer act as one of a committee appointed by the ladies, it will not do for me to put myself forward. Some may say, I take upon me more than I need to. We have to look all about us when there are so many different sorts of people to please."

This was all new to Lucy. " Ought I to ask any one else to help me ? " said she.

" There is the deacon's wife, Mrs. Silas, she would be delighted to go out with you."

"I am not very much acquainted with her,"
said Lucy, sighing.

"Never mind, then," said Mrs. Kennedy, "if
you wish it I am at your service, so do n't be one
grain troubled; I 'll see that it is all made right,"
— and they went out together.

Mrs. Kennedy managed so as to make Lucy's
money go far; she bought chiefly of their own
people, who gladly sold to their minister's wife at
cost. When all was completed, the day was fixed upon for the house-warming, and notice of it
given. All the Downs Street people were invited
to call upon their minister and his wife, at any
hour of the day or evening of the following Thursday.

Early on Monday morning, a little note from
Mrs. Silas arrived, saying, "that the ladies wished
to send in cake and other refreshments for the occasion, if it would be agreeable to the minister and
his wife."

Lucy did not know what to reply; she was perplexed by this proposal, for she had decided upon
a plan, which Mr. Holbrook had approved, — that
was, to offer their wedding cake to their guests;
and she did not like to change this arrangement
without consulting him, and as it was study hours,
she would not then interrupt him, so she deferred
replying to the note till noon.

In thinking over the proposal, Lucy did not altogether approve it. It seemed to her awkward, to invite their people to their house, and yet permit them to bring their own refreshments, and Mr. Holbrook was inclined to take the same view of it. As they could not arrange it satisfactorily, he proposed to her to go around and get Mrs. Talbot's opinion of the proprieties in the case, and she went.

When she found herself standing alone on the steps of the great house, she felt somewhat timid, but no time was allowed her to dwell upon it, for her ring was immediately answered, and she was conducted up stairs, and ushered into a suit of superb rooms. In an easy chair, before a bright wood fire which blazed in the back parlor, sat Mrs. Talbot. She was reading when Lucy entered, but immediately put down her book and received her guest with great cordiality.

At first, Lucy was awed by the splendor around her, for she had never seen the like before ; she felt less at her ease with Mrs. Talbot than she had done in the little parlors of " Number Five ;" style seemed to come between them, and she hesitated about introducing the object of her call. But Mrs. Talbot's manner soon re-assured her, so that she spoke without hesitation of the little difficulty which had arisen, and Mrs. Talbot entered into it with unaffected interest.

"Your plan of simply offering your wedding cake," said she, "would have been very appropriate, if the ladies had not appeared anxious to provide the entertainment themselves; but since they have done so, if I were you, I would accept the attention."

She then entered fully into the detail of the arrangements, telling Lucy how and where to set her tables, and offered to send her own man to act as waiter, a service to which he was accustomed. Lucy left her, much relieved.

Through Mrs. Kennedy the ladies were informed that their offer would be acceptable, and, on Tuesday, large supplies of cake began to pour in. Young ladies, with sparkling eyes and bright cheeks, were on the wing, continually coming, depositing their cargo of sweets, then flying off again, and by Thursday morning Mrs. Holbrook's china-closet was laden. At an early hour in the morning, Mrs. Talbot's man came, and went at once to work. By Lucy's direction he set the table in the study. Lucy soon saw that John was in his element, and understood the matter of arranging tables better than she did; she therefore left it wholly to him.

John made his own selections from the cake in the china-closet, laying by each dish the card which accompanied it, when he could conveniently do so. He displayed both taste and skill, and when he had given the finishing touch to his table, it looked elegantly. Mr. Holbrook and Lucy were standing and admiring it, when Mrs. Kennedy came in.

"What! all through so soon," said she; "why, I came to help you. O, the table looks beautifully!"

"John must be thanked for it," said Mrs. Holbrook.

"John? O yes; well, John, have you put on all the cake?"

"No, ma'am," said he, "there is as much more in the closet; but then most of it is plain. I've got all that's frosted."

"Ah! John," said Mrs. Kennedy, laughing, "I am afraid that will never do. I'll go and look; it won't do to hurt people's feelings, you know; we had better hurt our table."

Mrs. Kennedy looked into the china-closet. "Here," said she, "is a plate of sugar gingerbread from Mrs. Wood, a poor washer-woman; I dare say, she sat up half the night to make it, for she thinks everything of her minister. We must not leave this out on any account. Here are buns from the Pelham's, — sewing-girls they are, who have no home of their own, but very worthy girls. Here, John, we must find room for the buns, too."

"Indeed, madam," said John, "there is no room; the table is full,— very full."

"I'll tell you what we can do," said Mrs. Kennedy, lifting up two silver baskets of her own elegant cake, "mine will keep, Mrs. Holbrook; just slip it into your cake-box; you will find it convenient by and by, and we will put the buns and gingerbread here. That is," said she, after a pause, "if you approve."

"Certainly," replied Lucy, "I would not have any of our people feel slighted; it is to be their day, and we must do what will best please them."

John made the exchange, gravely and reluctantly. Just then the door bell rang, and he took his station below. It was Mrs. Talbot, who had come to see what progress was made. John went up stairs with her to show her his table, and Mrs. Holbrook told the story of his choosing the handsome cake, and of Mrs. Kennedy's reasons for the exchange. John stood in the entry, hearing this, and, looking in and laughing, secretly hoping his mistress would side with him, and advise the restoration of that elegant cake, the pride of his table. Mrs. Talbot disappointed him; she told Lucy, "by all means to do honor to the gifts of the poor," so John was obliged to leave his treasure in the cake-box.

Ring — ring — ring, — the people meant to

honor their pastor's invitation. And first came the aged ladies, who wished, in their call, to anticipate the crowd. Mr. and Mrs. Kennedy introduced those who were still strangers to the minister and his wife, and Lucy found herself among many new friends. She was glad to see them, and easily expressed this pleasure; but when the first greeting was over, she found a difficulty which she had not anticipated, in conversing with so many different people. She did not know what topics of conversation would interest them, and many times was forced to be silent.

Such was not Mr. Holbrook's experience. He was not now the shy, awkward student, in a rusty coat, and ragged collar, — but an ordained pastor, appropriately dressed, and moving about among his own people, who already regarded him with respect and affection. This new position inspired him with confidence, and he exhibited a versatility of address and fruitfulness of resources which he had never developed before. Lucy glanced at him now and then, and wondered. Was he, and that shy friend whom she knew at S., one and the same? She could hardly believe it. Once, it required an effort on his part to converse with a single stranger; now, he was entertaining a crowd. Such a change had necessity wrought in him. Lucy felt that she must rally her failing courage, and she went and sat down on the sofa by some old ladies who had been thus far, left pretty much to themselves.

" Do you enjoy good health ?" said she, kindly, to one whose face was much wrinkled and time-worn.

" Tol'able," she replied, " seeing I am hard on to eighty. But my race is e'en a'most run; I expect my summons now, every day. My sister had her summons about a month afore she died. I suppose you never hee'rd o'nt," said she, fixing a singular eye on Lucy.

" No," said Lucy, frightened, she scarcely knew why. In addition to the cadaverous expression of the old lady's countenance, there was something mysterious in her tone and manner which indicated that she was about to make an uncommon revelation.

" Well, — she was summoned," continued she, " and I expect to be. It was about four o'clock one winter morning. Dreadful cold it was; the wind blowed and roared down the chimney, and the blinds rattled. I lay in my bed, which it might be stood there in this corner, with the head agin the window, and the wooden shetters were shet. Well, the clock had just struck four, when there came three sich raps, as I guess you never heerd, right agin that shetter, and upon that our light went out.

My sister, says she to me, says she, — ‘ Hannah, that ’s my warning; I never shall do nothing more.’ Says I, ‘ I am afeard it is.’   We lay still, ’til the morning broke, then I got up, but sister — she could n’t lift her head, and she never did lift it again; she died in jest four weeks.   When she lay a dying, she says to me, in a very solemn tone, ‘ Hannah,’ says she, ‘ when your time is a coming I ’ll warn you.’   Now I am a looking for it every day, for Hannah was always as good as her word.”

“ That was very remarkable,” said Lucy, half-frightened; she did not know how to continue the conversation.   Mrs. Kennedy, observing her, came in a few minutes, and took her away from the old lady, into a little circle of young mothers, who had stolen out while their babies were sleeping. To Lucy it seemed like coming from a tomb into a merry nursery, and she was delighted with the young mothers, and they with her.

Ring — ring — ring still, — all the morning, all the afternoon, and by evening “ Number Five” was crowded with the Downs Street people.

John’s table was cleared before sundown, and, finding Mrs. Kennedy, he begged the handsome cake for his second table, and obtained it.   By nine o’clock this was also cleared.

The evening drew to its close, and Mr. Holbrook, taking a position at the foot of the stairs, thanked his people in a simple and appropriate manner, for their kind and generous attentions to him, expressed his pleasure at meeting so many of them, and his deep interest in their welfare. He then offered a prayer, and the people dispersed.

When Mr. and Mrs. Kennedy, the last lingerers, had said "good night," John went about with quiet tread, extinguished the lights, and then as quietly departed; and the minister and his wife were left alone, too weary, one would suppose, to think of making a second such effort very soon again. Yet the next morning, when Lucy saw the abundance of cake still remaining, a bright thought struck her; "why not invite the children of the society to meet their pastor?" She would do so, and accordingly it was done; and an afternoon was devoted to their entertainment.

Mr. Holbrook was pleased to meet the children, but Lucy was more than pleased, — she entered into their sports with as much glee as any of them, and they thought they had a fine time of it.

There was one little fellow, with large blue eyes, who claimed the minister as his particular property; his name was Herbert. When Mr. Holbrook sat down, he came, without fear, and climbed upon his knee; he put his arms about his neck, and kissed him. "I love you," said he. "Why?"

said Mr. Holbrook. "Because you are my minister."

When Mr. Holbrook walked about, Herbert ran at his side; and if he could not get a hand, held fast to his coat. When the cake was passed, his share he broke in two, and gave the larger piece to his minister. Lucy laughed heartily at this.

"You must adopt him, Charles," said she.

"I hope to adopt them *all*," said he, with much feeling. "I used to think, if I ever became a pastor, I should make a great deal of the children. We must nourish our buds, if we wish for choice fruit."

"I love you," said little Herbert again. The minister stroked his curly head, and seating himself in the midst of his flock, told them Bible stories. After this, he asked the children if they could sing. They could sing some Sabbath School songs which Lucy knew, so she stood a little aside from the group, and commenced singing. Soft young voices chimed in, and innocent eyes rested upon the minister, who seemed like a good shepherd among the lambs of his fold. When the music ceased, he prayed fervently. Nothing had occurred since his ordination which made him feel so sensibly that he was a *pastor*, as the look in those innocent eyes. It seemed to him to be no

trifling part of his new duties to influence young
children; to lure the feet of those little ones,
whose "journey was but just begun," into that
strait and narrow path, which leads to eternal
life; and he prayed that this duty might never be
neglected or despised.

CHAPTER IX.

GOING INTO SOCIETY.

SOME little time after the house-warming, Mr. and Mrs. Holbrook received an invitation to a large party. They had as yet gone but little into city society, and were not acquainted with the formalities which the case required. Lucy had, for some time, been wishing to take a present to John, as an expression of their appreciation of his services, and she thought this would afford her a good excuse for calling upon Mrs. Talbot, from whom she could learn just those things about a city party which she would be expected to know. Accordingly she went, and, as usual at that hour, found Mrs. Talbot reading in her easy chair. She was received kindly, and before long, was induced to speak of the real object of the call. Mrs. Talbot had also received an invitation to this party, and when she found how matters stood with her young friend, she decided, though contrary to her habits, to go out on that evening with her. She told Lucy that she would do so, and would call for her. Mrs. Talbot made a great effort to go out, for she was an invalid, but she made the effort with a sincere desire to benefit the new comers; yet she was not aware how great a kindness she was conferring upon them. Introduced by her, the minister and his wife made their first entrance into city society with a quiet self-possession which otherwise they would not have felt; they knew they could safely follow, where she led the way.

During the evening Lucy was, at one time, standing in a corner, silent; near her was a timid young lady, who was, also, a stranger. Pretty soon, Mrs. Talbot approached her, and said, in a low voice: "My dear, had you not better entertain that young lady, she seems less at home than yourself."

Lucy turned to reply, but Mrs. Talbot, smiling, moved quietly away. Lucy profited by the hint so delicately given. At the appointed hour, John came, and Mrs. Talbot, with Mr. and Mrs. Holbrook, took their leave. Lucy felt that if invited again to a city party, attendance would be a less formidable task, for she had, through the evening, carefully observed Mrs. Talbot, and had learned much from her.

"I did not see any of our people there," said Lucy, as they were riding home.

7

"I did not," replied Mr. Holbrook.

"I suppose," said he, hesitatingly, "that we have not many fashionable people among us."

This was new to Lucy; she did not understand the nice distinctions of city society. Mrs. Talbot understood better than either of them the relative position of the Downs Street Church, though, of course, she in no way manifested this knowledge.

As the evening was dark, and John was a wonderfully careful driver, it was late when the minister and his wife found themselves set down at "Number Five." Bridget was asleep in her chair, and Mr. Holbrook rang several times before he could waken her. "Ah, and indade," said she, by way of apology, "I was thinking it was the breakfast bell when you rung, and was going to make my coffee."

It was late, and Mr. Holbrook sat down by the fire and looked seriously at the coals.

"What is the matter?" inquired Lucy, "anything in there to trouble you?"

"No," said he, musingly, "but I cannot afford to give my time to parties; I have too much to do. We must have some rule about going out."

"We shall not be asked to go out often," said she, "we are invited now by Mrs. Talbot's friends because we are strangers. I dare say, our people never give parties."

"I do not think they do," replied he, "and if I knew this visiting would last but for a season, I would cheerfully devote some time to it, for I need to go more into society."

"How much more you are at your ease than you used to be," said Lucy. "Do you remember that evening in S.?"

"When I met Miss Hubbell?"

"Yes."

"Remember it! to be sure. I was thinking of it the other day, and of the collars you mended."

"Why do you not wear them now?" said Lucy, laughing.

"Do you wish me to?"

"No, for I do believe one reason why you feel more at your ease than you used to, is because you are better dressed."

"It may be so," was his reply.

After this night's dissipation, the morning had so far slipped away before Mr. Holbrook felt like rising and going to work, that he was led to adopt fierce resolutions against parties. Lucy thought them superfluous, for she hardly expected to be invited to another; yet, before long, a second invitation came. Mr. Holbrook wished to decline it; Lucy thought it prudent not to do so without first consulting Mrs. Talbot.

Now Mrs. Talbot knew the lady from whom

the invitation came, and that it was her custom to give parties only for ministers; and also that she was particularly attentive to such as were strangers. She thought one object in her giving a party at that time, was to introduce the Downs Street minister and lady; she therefore urged their going, and again kindly insisted upon sending her carriage. To this Lucy would not consent; "the evening was fine, and they should prefer walking."

"Well," said Mrs. Talbot, opening a drawer as she spoke, and taking out a pair of soft, coarsely knit stockings, "draw these on over your others before you go out, your feet will be too thinly dressed for walking."

When Mr. Holbrook heard Lucy's report he looked grave; what would become of his fierce resolutions if he went? yet it seemed necessary that the invitation should be accepted, and he, reluctantly, consented.

Mrs. Talbot was right in her opinion of the party; it had been given for ministers, to most of whom Mr. and Mrs. Holbrook were yet to be introduced. Lucy felt like a stranger among them; but remembering Mrs. Talbot's example, she endeavored to be social with those immediately about her.

The evening was passing more pleasantly than

she had at first anticipated, when a venerable, white-haired clergyman, who had been eyeing her for some time, approached, and was introduced as Dr. Graves.

He was a man of kind feelings, who was particularly anxious to make himself serviceable to every young minister, or young minister's wife, who fell in his way ; he thought all such could profit by his long and varied experience.

In a very formal way, he commenced conversation on general subjects. Pleased with the freshness and simplicity of his new acquaintance, — he was soon led into particulars.

" The duties of a minister's wife are new to you, I suppose, my dear."

" Yes, sir."

" Doubtless, you find them very arduous, but they are also exceedingly gratifying when rightly performed.

" Yes, sir," said Lucy, again, but that was too short, and she added, " I am but a new beginner."

" Well, my dear," continued he, " if you give yourself up, heart and soul, to your work, you will be guided safely. You have only to endeavor to set your people such an example in all things, as it will be safe for them to follow."

" Yes, sir," said Lucy, looking rather blank.

" It will give me great pleasure," continued the

7*

old gentleman, " to introduce you to a friend of
mine, Mrs. Lacy. She is a perfect pattern of a
Christian woman. She lends herself wholly to
every good work ; ' in season, and out of season;'
she, indeed, ' does with her might whatsoever her
hands find to do.' If you can become acquainted
with her, and copy her in some of these things,
you will be eminently useful in your new position ; let me introduce you to her."

" No, no, Dr." said a well known voice ; " we
want our minister's wife to be herself, and copy
after no one. Mrs. Lacy is a charming woman,
but we all like to have our own ways of doing
good."

" Ah, Mrs. Kennedy ! is that you ? Indepen-
dent as ever, I see," said the old gentleman, smiling.

Lucy turned, and grasped Mrs. Kennedy warmly
by the hand ; indeed, she did not leave her again,
through the evening. She felt shy of such of the
clergy as showed the " blossoms of the almond-
tree ; " she feared further enlargement on the awful
responsibilities of her new position ; she scarcely
dared raise her eyes to that part of the room
where Mrs. Lacy stood, lest she should see such
glowing perfection as would completely over-
whelm her.

The old Dr. walked away and entirely forgot
his benevolent plan of making them acquainted,

but he left poor Lucy full of serious thoughts, not
the most appropriate for the socialities of a drawing-room.

What was before her? Was she expected to
be a "living example, known and read of all?"
She, — but just from school, new to herself and
all the world! Was not she yet a learner in all
things; how then could she teach? Mrs. Kennedy observed the thoughtful expression of her
countenance, and kindly broke up her misgivings,
with many domestic inquiries. Did Bridget answer their purpose? How did their coal burn?
— and the study stove, was it the thing they
needed there?

Lucy answered these inquiries, and as she entered into the subject, the clouds began to dis-
perse; yet she was not sorry when the evening
had passed. Such a body of clergymen appeared
very formidable to her; it was a grave matter to
look upon them, and to feel that her young pastor
had now joined their ranks, and had his position
yet to take among them; she wondered what it
would be.

As she passed through the hall on her way out,
she saw Dr. Graves again. Afraid that by some
accident he might be thrown into their company
in their homeward walk, she slipped quickly
through the outer door, and would have gone

down the steps with a fall, had not some one caught her. It was John, who was waiting there with his carriage; for it had commenced raining, and Mrs. Talbot had sent him. Lucy felt as if she had a mother in Mrs. Talbot, and as if John also belonged to them. Early the next morning, before commencing the business of the day, she slipped over to tell her about the party, and of her interview with Dr. Graves.

CHAPTER X.

THIS second party was also followed by a broken morning, which Mr. Holbrook was too wise again to mend with "resolutions." He thought it over in silence; for he was earnestly seeking knowledge as to what a city minister's life is, and what it can be made. To him it was an unsolved problem; how was he to do justice to himself, and yet do justice to his people. Thus far, his miscellaneous duties had scarcely left him time even for sermon-writing, but he hoped that when he ceased to be a new man in his place, many interruptions would cease.

Lucy was enlivening a fragment of the morning, by a graphic account of her interview with Dr. Graves, when Mrs. Kennedy called. Her object was, to inquire if Lucy would accept the office of president of the Sewing Society; the ladies were very anxious that she should do so.

Mr. Holbrook answered for her; "No," said he, decidedly, "Mrs. Holbrook ought not to undertake anything more. It is not necessary that she should be burdened with the care of my people. I am

sure that she will do all for them that she can con-
sistently with her other duties and her health, and
more than this ought not to be expected of her. I
am not at all of Dr. Graves's mind, that she must
be made a martyr, for the sake of becoming an
example."

Lucy, who was sitting in the corner of the sofa,
laughed merrily at this burst of eloquence, for
which she seemed indebted to Dr. Graves. She
was glad no one but Mrs. Kennedy heard it, for
it would have been an easy thing to have mis-
represented what was said; Mrs. Kennedy she
knew was a prudent friend, and would not repeat
anything which might be turned to their injury.

Mrs. Kennedy had no disposition to report this
remark. She had lived longer in the world than
Mr. Holbrook, and knew that time would modify
such opinions, or, at least, change the expression of
them. It was not the first instance she had met,
of a minister's being chary of his young wife, and
she could make allowances for him. She took
good care that no trouble should ensue from
Lucy's declining the office.

Before long, the anniversary of an important
local society called the minister and his wife out
on another evening. When they arrived at the
church it was late, and they quietly entered a side
slip. The house was well filled, and the platform

crowded with clergymen. Some of them were literally "*watchmen* on the walls of Zion," for with eyes fixed on the ever opening door, they noticed all who entered. Mr. Holbrook did not take his seat unobserved; neither was he long left unmolested. The watchman came down, and held a conversation with him at the pew door. Mr. Holbrook looked disturbed; his brother ministers insisted upon his making an address in the place of an absentee. Lucy plainly read his distress as he went to the platform. He was awkward at extemporaneous speaking; he had never appeared before such an audience; he was called upon to speak without preparation on a subject, the local bearings of which he did not understand. These circumstances combined, made it a serious trial to his feelings, and it was with a nervous tread, and flushed countenance, that he went up and took his seat among his veteran colleagues. Trial as it was, however, he well knew that from it there was no honorable retreat. The life of a city minister is a life of *emergencies* to which he must be always equal. " Let no man despise thy *youth*," was an apostolic injunction of which Mr. Holbrook often thought; now he must obey it. Poor Lucy seemed to know his feelings by instinct, and sympathized fully with them. Her heart beat violently; tears came to her eyes; she wished she had stayed at home.

" Bless his heart," said a soft voice back of her,
" it is too hard to make him go up there."

" Never fear for him," was the quick reply, in a
well-known voice.　Lucy turned, with a grateful
look, and Mrs. Kennedy bowed and smiled, — so
the tears stood in the young wife's eyes, and did
not drop.

During the prayer, and the reading of reports,
Mr. Holbrook concentrated his thoughts on the
work before him.　True, he knew but little of its
peculiar claims.　But he knew, that strike a vein
of true benevolence where you will, it will be
found flowing directly from the great heart of
Christian love.　On this he could speak, and waving all apology, with this he commenced.　At first
he spoke with difficulty ; his voice often trembled ;
his glances over the great audience were transient ;
his manner was diffident ; but necessity was upon
him, and the reverence which he felt for the
preacher's work, drew forth in this emergency the
power that was in him.　As he warmed with his
subject, words began to flow ; and soon he almost
forgot the great audience, in his earnestness to do
his Master's work.　In this desire his diffidence
subsided into a manly modesty, and he spoke as
one invested with authority.　When his address
was completed, a general movement and ex-
changing of glances expressed the agreeable sur-

prise of the audience, while the bowed heads of some indicated that hearts had been touched.

" I told you so," said Mrs. Kennedy, triumphantly, to her neighbor.   Lucy again turned, but now she was smiling, though even when the clouds were gone and the sun fairly shone, those wayward tears, like wayward showers in April, must needs fall.

This evening's adventure excited Mr. Holbrook, and gave him a wakeful night; the consequence was another broken morning. Its results, however, were important to him; it served as an introduction to the community, and gave him a place among the ministers. Lucy, also, was led by it to consider it desirable that one of them, at least, should attend public meetings frequently, and she resolved that she would go whenever any meetings of importance were held in the day.

Before long, she had an opportunity to attend a quarterly meeting of a Children's Friend Society. It was to be held in the morning, and therefore she was obliged to hasten away, and leave Bridget in charge of all the dinner arrangement, which she had been prevented from making by an early visitor. As she was walking rapidly to the vestry, she heard some one call her, from a carriage, and Mrs. Talbot looked from the window, and invited her to ride.

Lucy excused herself on the plea, "that she was going to meeting." Mrs. Talbot said, "she would take her there."

"You are out early," said Mrs. Talbot, when they were seated together.

"Yes, very early," said Lucy, "but I thought I ought to go. I had company before breakfast was over, and I could not get time to see to anything. I do not know what will become of my house; I have to neglect it. Sometimes I think it would have been better for us to have boarded."

"Do not feel troubled, my dear," said Mrs. Talbot, "your work will arrange itself by and by, so that it will all come easier, and you will also become accustomed to it. We are not required to do any more than we can do, and you will soon learn to be content with this."

John stopped at the vestry of Dr. Graves's church, and interrupted a pleasant conversation. "O dear," said Lucy, with a cheerful laugh, for her spirits had risen as their burden had been lightened; "O dear, if Dr. Graves himself is there, what shall I do?"

John looked up at her with a serio-comical expression of countenance, as if he appreciated her feelings, and yet had a joke ready to crack in his teeth at the Doctor's expense. John and Mrs. Holbrook were fast becoming friends.

Lucy entered the vestry, and the first thing which she saw was Dr. Graves, in the pulpit. She quietly took her seat, and endeavored to listen to the remarks which followed his prayer; but they interested her less than the novel scene of a morning assembly, composed entirely of ladies. She did not understand how so many of them could leave home at that hour.

Dr. Graves having concluded his remarks, took his departure, and much to Lucy's surprise, Mrs. Lacy, clad in velvet and sable, rose, and took his place. In a graceful and dignified manner, she took charge of the meeting, and managed its business. Lucy still looked upon her with wonder; she, certainly, was a remarkable woman; and she felt more fear of her than ever. How could she stand up before so many people and address them? Had Lucy been called upon to do it, she certainly would have fainted away. Thus reminded of her own inefficiency, her former misgivings returned to trouble her. How could she ever perform the duties of a city minister's wife? She half wished Mr. Holbrook had settled on the Green Mountains.

These thoughts were a little diverted as the exercises proceeded, and yet, when the meeting was over, Lucy was ready to hasten away, as if she could leave them behind. A lady stopped

her; — it was the lady at whose house she met
Dr. Graves, and she was immediately introduced
by her to Mrs. Lacy.   Lucy scarcely raised her
eyes.

"I have not seen you here before, I think,"
said Mrs. Lacy, kindly.   "No, I have never been
present before."

"I am happy to see you here, and it will give
me pleasure to introduce you to some of our leading members.   The wish has been expressed to
appoint you treasurer for the coming year."   "I
do not think —," said Lucy, blushing and hesi-
tating, and leaving her sentence unfinished.

"You cannot have our minister's wife," was
said by a pleasant voice.

"Take the office yourself, then, Mrs. Kennedy,"
replied Mrs. Lacy, turning quickly.   ·

"Not I, indeed," was the reply.   "I have my
hands full; you must give it to some young lady."

"Just find us one, if you please."   Lucy did
not wait for the final settlement of the matter, but
slipped out, and gladly turned her face homeward.   She had not proceeded far, when she
heard some one walking quickly behind her.   She
turned, and saw a lady whose face was familiar,
though her name was forgotten; yet, as she knew
her to be one of Mr. Holbrook's people, she felt
at liberty to shake hands with her, and inquire
after her family.

"They were all well, excepting Mr. Roberts; he had a bad cold." The lady, then, was Mrs. Roberts, and as she walked along with the minister's wife, she chatted on various subjects, and among other items of news, she said to her: "Yesterday I called on Mrs. Vinton, and I found both she and her husband felt hurt because Mr. Holbrook had not been to see them. They knew he had been at Mr. Baker's, and that's only a few doors from them; they never knew a syllable about the house-warming, until it was all over, and they were hurt about that too. And they say, 'if they are not of consequence enough to be taken any notice of, it's no matter how soon they leave, — they are thinking seriously of going to some other church.' I thought I would just tell you," said Mrs. Roberts, "for, perhaps, you and the minister might find time to run in before they go." "Certainly," said Lucy, "we will try to do so." She was finding out that shadows fall, even over the path of a city minister.

After leaving Mrs. Roberts, business detained her, and she did not reach home until dinner was on the table. She found Bridget had roasted a fresh piece of meat, of which there was no need, for there was plenty left from the dinner of the day before to have served them; but Lucy, in her haste to be off in season, had forgotten to

8*

speak of it, and Bridget had done as well as she knew how, and therefore was not to be blamed. Thus the fifty cents were not saved, because of the early quarterly meeting which the minister's wife must attend. Lucy's thoughts were so much occupied with Mrs. Lacy and Mrs. Vinton, that the little matter scarcely troubled her, and her husband insisted upon knowing why she looked so grave. She gave him the history of the morning. He laughed that she was disturbed because she did not understand parliamentary usage as well as Mrs. Lacy, but was himself disturbed at Mrs. Vinton's state of mind. He took out his visiting list, which, as yet, was only alphabetically arranged. True, Mrs. Baker lived in the same street with Mrs. Vinton, and he had called upon one, and not upon the other.

"I cannot go to see her this week," said he, "nor next either, I am afraid."

"I am sorry," said Lucy, "for she was over-looked in the house-warming, and has some reason to feel slighted. I met her once at Mrs. Kennedy's, and was pleased with her. I do not like to lose her. Do not you suppose you could save a few minutes just to run in with me before tea?"

"Possibly I may be able to; will you be all ready?"

"Yes," said Lucy.

"If I am not here at the appointed time, do not sit with your cloak on. I will be punctual if I can go at all."

The afternoon, if so we must dignify the short space between dining and dark, was soon gone, and the shadows of the brick houses fell black and heavy across the street; the appointed time passed, but Mr. Holbrook did not appear. Lucy sat a few minutes to consider. Should she venture out alone? Why not? She knew just about where Mrs. Vinton lived, and might soon be there. Yes, she would go. She walked quickly, that the darkness might not gain on her; found the street and the house, and was admitted to a back parlor, where Mrs. Vinton sat, undressing her baby. Lucy felt that her unseasonable call required some apology, for Mrs. Vinton looked surprised.

"I have come in very unceremoniously," said she, pleasantly. "Mr. Holbrook and I were coming in together, but he has been prevented, and I thought I would not get cheated out of my call. I have not seen you in a long time; you were not at our house-warming, nor Mr. Vinton either; I don't know but I shall call you to account for it."

"My dear Mrs. Holbrook," said Mrs. Vinton, "if you won't mind my baby, sit right down here, and let me tell you all about it."

Lucy heard the whole story, and then explained

to Mrs. Vinton how it came about that she had
not been called upon as soon as Mrs. Baker.

"Well, I never!" said Mrs. Vinton, when she
had heard her through, "we ought not to blame
our ministers until we know their side, as well as
our own; and yet, a great many of us do. For
my part, I never did it yet, without having something turn up to make me sorry for it afterwards."

Lucy was much pleased by Mrs. Vinton's frank-
ness, and quite cheerful again; she took up the
baby, to have a frolic with him. As she did so,
her glove fell almost into a dish of pears which
stood by the stove, warming for tea.

"What fine looking pears," said Lucy, as Mrs.
Vinton put them aside, "are they preserved, or
stewed?"

"Only stewed," said Mrs. Vinton; "husband
is very fond of them. Do eat some, will you?"

"No, I thank you," said Lucy, "but I should
like to know how you cook them."

Mrs. Vinton explained the process with evident
pleasure; she took a pride in nice cookery.

Darker and darker fell the huge shadows; now
Lucy certainly must go. She, therefore, kissed
the baby, shook hands with the mother, and they
parted good friends.

Darker it certainly was than when she came —
much. Here and there a lamp-lighter appeared

with his blazing torch. It was late for Lucy to be out alone, — in the city, too. She began to walk rapidly, and more and more rapidly as she heard steps behind her — a man's steps certainly, and now, nearer and nearer, in spite of her exertion, — a hand touched her shoulder. " Why, Lucy," was said just in time to prevent the scream which rose to her lips. Lucy was timid; she had exaggerated ideas of the wickedness which walketh in darkness.

" How you frightened me, Charles," she panted out.

" Where have you been at this hour, Lucy?"

" To call upon Mrs. Vinton," said she; " as soon as I get my breath, I 'll tell you about it, which she did accordingly. Mr. Holbrook felt that her call had done as much towards reconciling the disaffected as his own would have done, and, perhaps, even more. Of this he was convinced the next morning, for, before Bridget had her fire kindled, the door bell rang, and Mr. Vinton, who was on his way down town, called to leave a jar of stewed pears which Mrs. Vinton sent, with her love. Those pears, which with many repentant feelings at having unjustly blamed her minister Mrs. Vinton had sat up half the night to cook, linked her to him, and from that time the minister and his wife had no warmer friends than Mr. and Mrs. Vinton.

If you have aught against your minister, do not treasure it up, at least until you have heard *his side* of the difficulty. Is it a trifle, not important enough to mention to him, which troubles you? bring him then an offering, which is to you a *labor of love*, and it will set all right in your heart. This is what Mr. and Mrs. Vinton will tell you.

CHAPTER XI.

MAKING CALLS. A LETTER.

"DEAR MARY:—"I feel almost ashamed to write to you again,—your last unanswered letter dates so far back; but the simple truth is, the wife of a city minister has no time of her own. O, if I had only known this before I came! I think it would have scared away what little courage I had. To-day it storms, fortunately. I cannot get out, and no one can get in, so I have a chance to write you a few lines."

After describing to her friend their house, manner of living, etc., Lucy went on to give her an account of their making calls,—in the following:—

"I thought of you the other day, when I was getting ready to go out with Mr. Holbrook to call upon some of our people. As the street where we wished to go was at some distance from "Number Five," and I was not very well, we took a carriage for a few hours. I dressed in my best, and I thought we started off in great style. At many places we found the people absent, and, to tell the truth, our visiting list was so enormous, I was not sorry to have it reduced in any honest way. At one time we drove up a very narrow street, and entered a very old-fashioned house; here we found the family all at home. They had assembled to receive us in a plain parlor, the principal ornament of which was a stand of house-plants, mostly in bloom. The family party consisted of an old gentleman, his wife, and two young daughters; the latter so shy, they were afraid even of me! I was put upon my wits to keep up a conversation. I talked the flowers over, — stalk, stem, leaf, and bud, and to all my profound remarks I received only a whispered, — 'yes or no.' I began to realize what a great thing it is to be a minister's wife, when even *I*, as such, could *awe* people. It struck me comically; I felt as if I must laugh, but I did n't dare to. The old lady, after awhile, roused a bit. 'She would go into the other half of the house,' she said, 'and hunt up sister Nanny.' This she did, and on her return came and sat still nearer me. Her countenance wore its most Sabbath-day expression, and I could not look at it. 'Do you like the city?' she asked, in a very serious tone. 'Yes,' said I, 'and I presume I shall like it better and better as I become more accustomed to it.' 'You have never lived in one before?' 'No, — I am a country girl.' 'O! — well, do you know many of our folks?' 'Not very many yet, — I am getting

acquainted.'   Here came an awful pause.   I bit
my lip.   It seemed to me as if the old lady were
waiting for words of wisdom, to fall like honey
from my lips.   Now imagine me, Mary, if you
can, making wise remarks in a still room!   I looked over to Charles to see if the time of our departure was not near at hand.   He would n't look
at me, but kept on talking with the old gentleman,
whose tongue run like a mill-stream.   On our
side of the room a new topic was introduced; it
was Becky, — Becky, the eldest daughter; and
from this time the burden of the conversation was,
' that Becky had n't come, and she would be so
sorry to lose the call.'

"I saw now that a city minister's wife must
have *tact* as well as good feeling, or she will never
make friends with such a variety of people.   The
instant we rose to go, the spell of the parlor was
broken.   The family crowded together, followed
us to the door, — all talking at once, and telling
us how glad they were to see us, and begging us
to come again.   As we stood there, it struck me
we should make a fine group for a picture.   At
the parlor door was the old patriarch, with his
pale blue eyes and pleasant countenance, still talking fast to the young minister whom he held by
the hand.   By his side was his wife; the deep
lines in her countenance indicated that she had

9

passed through the checkered experience of a
long life. She was reverently listening to the
remarks of her husband, when, observing a little
spot upon his coat, she wet her finger and carefully rubbed it out without disturbing him.   Behind her, the young faces of her daughters, stretch-
ed away into the back-ground, all of them with
pale blue eyes, and the father's mild look. They
waited only for him to say his last word, when
they all broke in together with their say. Their
eyes sparkled; their faces lighted up, and even
aunt Nanny, who might properly be called 'homely
as time,' looked animated and lively. The kind
gladness of their hearts and voices was contagious,
it was excited by *love for their minister*, and came
bubbling up, as soon as parlor restraint was removed. I entered into full sympathy with it, almost before I knew it. ' Who would not choose
to be a minister,' thought I, 'and have a people
to love him.' When we went out, they followed
us even to the carriage steps. I sprang up, exhilarated by the scene, and feeling, with the old lady,
truly sorry ' that Becky was n't at home.' There,
Mary, — in spite of the rain I am interrupted, —
some one wishes to see me in the kitchen. If
anything occurs to detain me, so that I cannot
finish this sheet to-day, I shall send it just as it is.

Believe me, hurried or at leisure,

Ever your friend,   LUCY H."

CHAPTER XII.

THE SEWING SOCIETY.

IT was a poor girl who wished to see Mrs. Holbrook in the kitchen. She asked for work, but her manner and appearance were anything but prepossessing. Lucy had no work for her, and the girl went away angry. Mrs. Holbrook was leaving the kitchen, when Bridget detained her.

" Please, ma'am," said she, " could you ask Mr. Holbrook if I might go to his meeting?" I takes a sight of comfort in his prayers, and I should like to hear him preach."

" Certainly, you can go," said Mrs. Holbrook, " we should like to have you attend church and Sabbath school, both."

On the following Sabbath, Bridget, dressed in her best, which was every way respectable and neat, went to the Downs Street Church, and sat in the pastor's pew: Lucy was pleased to have some one there beside herself.

Early on Monday morning, Mrs. Kennedy called. " I was passing," said she, " and I thought I would run in. I want to speak about a little matter.

If Bridget would like to attend our meeting, Jane shall call for her every Sabbath. Perhaps it would be pleasant for them to sit together."

"Yes," said Lucy, hesitatingly, " where does Jane sit?"

" In a nice slip in the gallery," said Mrs. Kennedy; "you see very many of us could not afford to hire seats for our girls down stairs, and our galleries are free, and pleasant too. And," continued she, laughing, "if the minister's servants sit below, some of the others might feel themselves slighted, and that would make a little trouble, so I thought perhaps I had better just speak of it."

" I am glad you did," said Lucy, again. " I should indeed be sorry to do anything which would give the ladies trouble with their 'help.' If you will ask Jane to call, I will explain it to Bridget; she has good sense enough to understand the proprieties of the case."

" This is not all I came for," said Mrs. Kennedy; "our society begins this week. It meets on Wednesday evening at Mrs. Roberts. I told her I was coming by, and would stop and invite Mr. Holbrook and yourself."

" I do not think he can go," said Lucy.

" O yes, he can," said Mrs. Kennedy, " he must go, of course. We think everything of having our minister at our society meetings. It is the only time we all meet together socially, high and low, rich and poor. It would not be much without him."

A wayward thought suggested Mrs. Vinton to Lucy, and she told Mrs. Kennedy of the state of mind she had been in.

Mrs. Kennedy laughed ; " well, said she, " I am going near there, and I will just drop in, on my way, and let her know the society meets. We all like attention.

As Lucy had supposed, Mr. Holbrook felt as if he could not give up Wednesday evening, or any part of it, to the meeting of the Sewing Society. Since his settlement, he had not thus far, found time to read even the few periodicals for which he had subscribed. The evening was invaluable to him.

" It meets but once a month," said Lucy, persuasively. Mr. Holbrook consented to go, because it seemed necessary. They were quietly taking tea together before going out, when a little boy came in, to say that " Mrs. Lupin would call for Mrs. Holbrook, in a carriage, at an early hour."

" Does Mrs. Lupin keep a carriage ? " inquired Lucy, with some surprise, when the boy had left.

" No," replied the minister, " but Mr. Lupin sometimes drives a hack. You will go earlier

9*

than I shall ; gentlemen are not admitted until eight o'clock."

Lucy's brow clouded ; the idea of going without the minister was not pleasant to her. " Why may I not wait and walk with you ? " said she, in a beseeching tone.

" Mrs. Lupin would feel hurt, Lucy, and the ladies would be disappointed." " I wish she had not asked me to ride," thought Lucy, " for then I should have gone with him." With this feeling, she entered the carriage, half wishing she were not a minister's wife, and had n't to please every body.

But the little cloud of ill-humor, if it deserves so harsh a name, vanished at once in the friendly grasp of Mrs. Lupin's hand.

" This is a very cold evening, Mrs. Holbrook," said she ; " let me tuck you up in this buffalo ; husband put it in on purpose, so you need not feel the cold around your feet."

" You are very kind," said Lucy, " pray do not give yourself so much trouble ; I shall be warm enough, riding."

" Husband and I were talking about it," continued Mrs. Lupin, " and we concluded if you had to walk up to Mrs. Roberts's and back again, and stand all the evening besides, you would be clear

beat out. Now you must ride back too ; the carriage is to come on purpose."

This kindness touched Lucy. It was not after
all so bad a thing to be a minister's wife ; she resolved to do everything in her power to make the
evening pleasant to their people.

When once among them, she found herself the
object of such general attention that it embarrassed her. She was more than ready to be
eclipsed by the minister, who came at eight, and
to shine from that time as the lesser luminary. As
soon as it was proper, she made her way to his
side, and stood smiling at the enthusiasm which
his presence excited. The countenances of all,
both old and young, expressed pleasure. Beaming
eyes rested on him ; smiles everywhere met him,
while on soft cheeks the tell-tale color came and
went, at the notice or neglect of the young pastor.
He had come reluctantly to this society ; he did
mourn the loss of the hour ; he could not spare
it ; the dust was settling on his unopened books,
and how was he to live without study ? Once
there, however, these anxieties were forgotten ; he
thought not of his neglected studies, but of his
new charge. Heart answered to heart, for what
minister can withstand the affectionate interest of
his people ? Thus the evening passed, and at its
close, he stood in the midst of them and read the

hymn which they sung at parting, and sung, it would seem, with one mind, for in the prayer which followed, he bore them to the mercy-seat as his own.

When walking home, he asked himself, 'had not this interview with his people excited in him more enthusiasm for his morrow's task of sermon-writing, than even the projected evening's study would have done?'

A seat in the carriage in which Lucy rode home, had been reserved for the minister; but as he had slipped away unnoticed, Mr. Lupin occupied it.

Mr. Lupin was a plain, blunt man, of superficial attainments, but kind in his feelings, and active and stirring in his habits. He had a passion for enterprise. A keen, nimble, good-natured Yankee pedlar, would have served Mr. Lupin as an excellent model of a man.

Mrs. Holbrook had not before met him, but as he was one "who never stood on ceremony," they were soon acquainted.

"How crowded Mrs. Roberts's house was this evening," remarked Lucy, in the course of the conversation.

"Yes, there were a great many folks there," said Mr. Lupin, "and a great many there who won't go to meeting."

"I thought our church was well filled," remarked Lucy.

"Not half as full as it ought to be," said Mr. Lupin; "the fact is, we have been without a minister too long; 't will take us some time to fetch up. There is a great deal to be done."

"Our pastor is doing his share of it, I am sure," said Mrs. Lupin. "I know that," replied her husband, "but Mrs. Holbrook must help him about it. She must go about among the sick and the poor; she must take notice of this one and that one, whom nobody else will notice, and get them out; she must go and tell them the minister wants 'em to come and hear him preach, and flatter some folks up a little, especially the genteel folks, 't will do wonders for us."

Poor Lucy was silent, for she knew not what reply to make. Fortunately for her, Mrs. Kennedy was on the back seat, — she took up the glove.

"Now, Mr. Lupin, we do not expect our minister's wife to go about electioneering for her husband, and you must not try to make her think we do."

"Why no, not electioneering exactly, Mrs. Kennedy, but some one must fill up the church."

"For my part, I 've no fears but that we shall fill up fast enough while we have such preaching,"

said Mrs. Kennedy, "I've no fears; that will take
care of itself."

"Well, I do n't know," said Mr. Lupin, "there
are a great many pews yet to find market for.
They say Dr. Jay's church is crowded to overflowing, and there is n't a seat to be had, above
nor below. They've plenty of genteel folks, too.
Now, that is what we want."

Mrs. Kennedy was about to reply, when the
carriage stopped at "Number Five," and there
was only time to say "good-night." Lucy went
in, and sat down by the fire; Mr. Holbrook was
there; for a time but little was said.

"I do not know," remarked Lucy, breaking the
silence, "what I should do without Mrs. Kennedy."

"Why? what has happened now?" Lucy
repeated the conversation which had passed in
the carriage; and then it was Mr. Holbrook's turn
to look serious. He rose, and walked the room.
Almost every day was he learning something in
regard to the position of his church which surprised him. More than once had the opinion
been forced upon him by some little circumstance,
that it was on the decline, and that he had been
called to prop a falling house. Dr. Jay's church
was filled to overflowing, and why should not he
be as "popular" a preacher as Dr. Jay? With
this feeling, in one disguise or another, he fre-

quently came in contact. *Competition*, then, was the order of the day; competition must spur him to his sacred work; competition must darken those bright morning study hours; competition must steal away the light of those genial pastoral visits; competition must beckon him to that pulpit, which he had as yet never approached but with awe. He must come before his people like a stage-player, with clap-trap, and false thunder and lightning, to fill up the house! Was it to *this* work he had consecrated himself with solemn vows before God? Mr. Holbrook, in his momentary excitement, was fast drawing conclusions which his premises would not warrant. He did not wish to talk, but Lucy, observing his troubled brow, would not let him be silent.

"What disturbs you, Charles?" she asked. "The state of our church," said he, "I shall never answer their expectations, — I am not going to turn aside from what I consider my life's work, to court friends and sell pews."

"They do not wish you to do so," said Lucy, "no one has intimated such a thing but Mr. Lupin, that I know of."

"There is more of the feeling than you think for Lucy, but," continued he, with more calmness, "so far as I can see my path, it lies straight before me, and, I thank God, it is plain as daylight. I hope to walk in it, without turning to the right hand or the left. I will, to the best of my power, *preach the gospel.* To this I will devote myself. In my study, and in my pulpit, my people shall have my whole strength, whether I preach to many or few, — here or elsewhere, and to God will I trust my professional success; " and silently back and forth, — back and forth, he paced again.

"Well — " said Lucy, after awhile, poking the coals by way of companionship, " Mr. Lupin likes you, after all, I know."

" O yes, Mr. Lupin is a good friend of mine, and means well enough; I have received many kind attentions from him, but he is a man who must hear the wheel going round with a great splash, or he is not satisfied; silent revolutions he cannot understand."

" While your people crowd about you as they did to-night," said Lucy, " I think you have no reason to be discouraged."

" True," said Mr. Holbrook, coming now and sitting by her, "neither do I mean to be discouraged. I will do the best I can, and on that will I rest. But one thing I do wish, Lucy, and that is, that we could get along faster with our calls."

" I do too," said Lucy; "now, why cannot I make some without you ? " " I am afraid you

would not find it pleasant ; most of the people
are strangers to you."

"Never mind that," said Lucy, "only tell me
where to go, and whom to call upon, and let me
try it."

"I should be very glad to have you, if you
think you can," said the minister; "I will hand
you a list to-morrow."   He had already forgotten
what he had once told Mrs. Kennedy : "that he
belonged to the people, but Lucy to him."

10

CHAPTER XIII.

THE QUILLINGS.

LUCY received her list, and soon after went out without the minister, to make professional calls. This required an effort, for she was both new to the work, and a stranger in the city. A brisk walk of a few minutes brought her to the street which headed the list, and after travelling down one side of it, and nearly up the other, she came at last to the right number. It was some time before her ring was answered, and the door opened.

"Is Mrs. D. or her daughter in?" inquired she, of the person who appeared.

"Yes, I am her daughter." Lucy waited for an invitation to enter; no such invitation was given. The daughter stood awkwardly holding the half-closed door. If it had not been too late for Lucy to retreat, she might have done so, — but she stepped into the entry.

"It is Mrs. Holbrook," she said; "Mr. Holbrook wished me to call and see if you are all well. How is your mother? Can I see her?

"Yes, if you are a mind to," said the girl,

"she's down in the kitchen." "Shall I go down?" said Mrs. Holbrook, pleasantly. The girl stood aside to let her pass, and then vanished up stairs, for she felt awkwardly, and was mortified at being caught living in the kitchen. Lucy proceeded alone, and groping her way, she knocked at the first door she came to; that, as it happened, opened into the cellar, but further on was another, which was the right one, and at which the mother appeared, quite as much astonished as the daughter had been at seeing her minister's wife. Again Lucy felt that her presence required an apology, but Mrs. D. did not feel so ; she had just cleared up her kitchen, and was glad to see her visitor, and they sat down together by a little table under the basement window, and had a pleasant chat.

From this place, Lucy next entered a handsome house ; where she was ushered by a servant into pleasant parlors. She was wondering whether she should be here received as the stranger which she was, when the lady entered, and at once relieved her doubts, by the welcome which she gave her minister's wife. Soon the two ladies began to converse familiarly on domestic matters.

"You feel quite at home in the city now, I suppose?" said Mrs. Holbrook.

"I cannot say that I do," was the reply. "It is not very long since we moved in from the country, and to tell the plain truth, I cannot get acquainted in our society. We like our minister; but we find the people very different from those we left. To husband and me, they seem a little aristocratic and unsocial. No one has called on us since we came, and we have talked of going to a Methodist church. We were so used to having folks running in and out in the country, we miss it very much."

"Have you been to our Sewing Circle?" inquired Mrs. Holbrook. The lady had not.

"That is the place to get acquainted. You must go. It meets next week. You call for me on your way; I should like to introduce you to some of our people; I think you will like them."

The lady promised to do this, and when Mrs. Holbrook took her leave, she felt that she had certainly done good by this call.

In that street, three out of four of the families upon whom she called that afternoon, had recently moved in from the country. Under one form of expression or another, Lucy heard the same complaint from all. They felt lonely; they thought the Downs Street people unsocial; they missed the friendly running in and out of their country neighbors; they felt neglected, in short, for they were used to being made much of where they came from; important members they were of the churches they had left; it did come hard to settle down and be "nobody."

Mrs. Holbrook listened to these complaints, until her sympathies were roused. It seemed to her, the Downs Street people were remiss in their attentions to strangers, and needed chiding. Being near Mrs. Kennedy's, she ran in there on her way home, to see what she thought of it.

"The same old story," said Mrs. Kennedy, after listening quietly to the account; "and now, Mrs. Holbrook, I'll tell you just how it is; the Downs Street people are not inattentive to strangers; they are remarkably good about calling; but you see there is no such thing as pleasing every body, and of all the strangers whom we try to please, these country folks are the most difficult. They come here where everything is new; our customs, hours, and habits, all are strange to them, and they feel homesick, and miss their old neighbors. They are disappointed because we don't run in and out as they did, and set us down as aristocratic and reserved, and all that. Now you see everything is different in the country; there, they dine at twelve o'clock, and clear up and have the afternoon to go a visiting in; or, if not then, they have tea before sundown, and get the children off to bed, and take their knitting and run in and spend their evenings together. Here we dine late, and have

10*

no afternoons.   We take tea late, and then there
is always a meeting or a lecture in the evening
which our people wish to attend, and there is no
time, in the city, to run in and spend an hour
chatting with your neighbor.   If you go, you must
make a business of it, and take the time.   After
awhile our new comers find this out, and get wont-
ed to our ways; but before that, they pretty generally feel slighted, and keep moving about from
one church to another, hoping to find one that
is n't ' aristocratic,' as they call it, — but they do n't
succeed."

   " Well," said Lucy, " you know more about it
than I do, but I like the ladies I have seen this
afternoon.   I do not want to have them run away."

   " O, I will call upon them," said Mrs. Kennedy,
" and get Mrs. Silas to go with me.   I make it a
rule to call upon all whom I do hear of, but if
more move in next week and move out again,
before we have had a chance to hear of them, you
must not be surprised."

   Lucy, on her return, related her experience to
Mr. Holbrook.   " Mrs. Kennedy is right," said he,
" the ideas of sociality with which our country
friends come among us cannot be met, and their
unreasonable expectations and consequent disappointment are a great evil.   I hear of more dis-
content and complaint from them, than from any
other one class."

" Is there no help for it ?" inquired Lucy.

" None but time and patience, that I see."

Lucy's first effort at making professional calls had been so successful, she was encouraged by it to devote much of her time to this object, more indeed than she could well spare. To make amends for this, she was obliged to hire sewing done, which otherwise she would have done herself. Many expenses were incurred in the kitchen which need not have been, had she been, there to superintend ; but work will be done at a disadvantage, when the head of an establishment is away, — and the minister's wife must be away making calls. Had not Mr. Lupin said, " the folks must be called on ?" Mr. Lupin did not consider, that Mrs. Holbrook's time was money to her ; but it was, for all that. Such are some of the little leakages through which the minister's salary drops away bit by bit. His people, who reckon it by the hundreds, cannot for the life of them imagine where it all goes to so fast, — but away it goes, notwithstanding. They never reckon up the silver fractions of a dollar, which slip away, daily, in order to purchase time for the minister and his wife to devote to their service.

Yes, Lucy was needed at " Number Five," and she knew it, yet on this account she did not falter in her purpose of helping the minister by sharing the labor of making calls. She made one call, after awhile, which disturbed her equanimity. It was upon Miss Quilling. Mrs. Quilling had taken a house in the vicinity of the Downs Street Church, and her family accordingly had taken seats there as a matter of convenience. She had not much to do with it; she was old and infirm, seldom went out, and had become a cipher in her establishment. Lucy called there at Mr. Holbrook's request. She was shown up stairs into a small parlor, furnished with showy, but faded finery. Mrs. Quilling had once been rich, she was now reduced in her circumstances, and the family had not preserved much from the wreck of former days but their pride. This commodity they had treasured and transferred quite uninjured to their new abode, — that is, Miss Quilling and her brother had done so. As to the poor old lady, she was about dead to all the emotions which stir the living heart.

Our artless friend was awed when the majestic Miss Quilling, followed by her equally majestic brother, sailed into the room. Neither did this awe diminish when they seated themselves to converse, and informed Mrs. Holbrook just how long they had been members of Dr. Jay's church, and what important members too, — and how very full Dr. Jay's church was, and how very fashionable. They also very condescendingly expressed their interest in Mr. Holbrook, and their wish that he should call upon them without delay. Lucy became impressed with the feeling, that they were doing the Downs Street Church a great honor by coming there. Only to think of any of Dr. Jay's people joining them! She felt that no time should be lost in sending the minister and Mrs. Kennedy to call upon them. *They* must receive attention at all hazards, for were they not very genteel, and did not Mr. Lupin say, " they must get in genteel people?" As soon as Lucy reached home she found the minister, and told him how important it was that he should call upon Miss Quilling. " Shall I go to-night?" said he, putting down his pen, and laughing. Lucy looked astonished. " Why, no, — not to-night, but to-morrow."

" To-morrow," said he, " is devoted to the sick and afflicted. If Miss Quilling has so many warm friends in Dr. Jay's church, she will not be likely to suffer for want of attention."

Lucy colored, for this cool reply did not suit precisely her view of the case. In a moment, however, the transient vexation passed off, and she could laugh too. She was inclined to think the Downs Street Church would not fall quite asunder if anything should occur to send the Quillings elsewhere.

CHAPTER XIV.

THE MATERNAL MEETING.

ALTHOUGH, as the days slipped by, many names were struck from the 'calling-list,' it still remained formidable, and this was only one of many miscellaneous duties which consumed the minister's time. There was a great variety of meetings to be attended, and the maternal meeting stood among the foremost. To this, he was always especially invited; and attended somewhat unwillingly. Not that his interest in his little charge had at all diminished; but the truth was, so many years had passed since he had been intimate with childhood, that he found it difficult to express his interest in such a way as to awaken their sympathies. This was much increased by being called upon to speak when the mothers were present. He could talk to them when they were seated upon his knee, much more to the point than he could address them from the desk. For this reason, the notice of the meeting of a Maternal Association was usually the precursor of a perplexed hour. At length he received such a notice with entirely new feelings, and he began to pace back and forth in his study, earnest and excited. The little children seemed nearer and dearer to him than ever before; when he spoke to them, it was from the heart. There was a tenderness of feeling towards them which would gush forth. Now he was linked to them by a strangely new tie, for a little " birdie" was cooing in his own nest, and he, too, was a parent.

When Mrs. Kennedy, who slipped in after the minister, circulated this good news, there was great rejoicing at the maternal meeting. Mothers looked glad, and children's eyes sparkled, and when the services were over, all crowded around the young father with inquiries and congratulations. He forgot, in the joy with which the little one was welcomed, that she was born into a world of sin, and that no earthly love could bear for her, her share of its sorrows. Finding himself quite overcome, he was hastening home, when he was stopped by some one pulling his coat. He turned, and saw Herbert. His blue eyes were opened to their widest extent, his face was flushed, and he lisped out, as well as in his haste he could, " Mr. Holbrook, may I go and see the little baby?"

" Yes, — some time you shall," said Mr. Holbrook, kindly; " come next week." Herbert dropped his hold of the coat and turned away. There

was such a sudden change from animation to sorrow in his expressive countenance, that it touched
the minister's sympathy.

"Well, Herbert," said he, "take hold of my
hand, and we will go and see about it."

Herbert was all sunshine again, and ran, talking and jumping, until he reached the door of
"Number Five;" he then went up softly into the
study, and the minister as softly entered the adjoining room. After some little parleying with
the nurse, the "wee thing," carefully wrapped in
a blanket, was put into its father's arms, and made
its first journey. The corner of the blanket was
turned down, and Herbert peeped in, laughing
heartily at the queer faces the baby seemed making up at the world it had entered.

Before night, Herbert had told every Downs
Street child he met that he had seen the baby.
The next morning, while Mr. Holbrook was taking
his breakfast, two little girls came on the same
errand. One brought a wax doll, and the other
a basket of sugar-plums, and they wished to go
up stairs ; and so it turned out, that the "wee
thing," having made one journey, was obliged to
repeat it very often.

The minister, being interested in new scenes,
and occupied with new joys and new cares, found
he could not regulate his hours as he had once

done. He was obliged to make frequent exchanges; and yet he gave no time to any duty about his house which he could hire done. It was not strange, therefore, taking into account the heavy expenses of the season, that, at the end of the year, he found himself considerably in debt; but it was a trial for which he was unprepared. While obtaining his education, his means of living had been so very limited, that the sum of fourteen hundred dollars he thought amply sufficient for the support of his family, and he had not therefore troubled himself about economizing. But in this, " he had reckoned without his host;" for, when the year came round, he was convinced that on two points he had been quite in the dark, — one was, the expense of living in a city, and the other was, the expense of house-keeping at all. It was a gloomy day to him when his bills came in, and he discovered how much he had miscalculated. Indeed, he was so much disturbed, he could not study; he left his books, went into the nursery and told Lucy of his perplexity. If she had been well, she would have taken the trouble on a buoyant wing; but in her feeble state, it depressed her. She began to mourn that " she was unable to be about and see to things." Mr. Holbrook, therefore, returned to his room, resolved to bear this little burden alone.

11

On the evening of this day he was to have a conference-meeting, for which it was necessary that he should make more than usual preparation; but he was so dispirited that he had serious thoughts of changing the character of the meeting, and asking one of the deacons to take his place. Yet this was but a momentary surrender to his trouble, — he soon summoned his energy, resolved to do *present* duty, and trust for the morrow.

He prepared for and attended the meeting. Feeling more exhausted than usual after it, he was about leaving the vestry, silently and hastily, when Mr. Kennedy touched his arm.

"I will detain you but a moment, sir," said he, — "a little business." Mr. Kennedy's face was lighted up, — something evidently pleased him; he hemmed once or twice, and then with a smile drew an envelope from his pocket.

" Some of our people, sir, thought your expenses this season must have been heavy, and they wished me to hand you this."

Mr. Holbrook opened the envelope, and found enclosed a hundred dollars. One hundred dollars! how timely, — was ever present more so? Was ever a people more generous than Mr. Holbrook's? Never, he thought, for most liberally had they anticipated and provided for difficulties which he

had not forethought enough in such matters to fore-
see. This seemed to him a remarkable act of generosity. He compared it with the tardy and limited
gifts of some of whom he had heard, — dwellers
in parts of the country where money circulates less
freely, and where a hundred dollars is thought
about enough for the support of a minister and
his family for the year. It seemed to him, that
his people had done a great thing for him, — and
so they had. He recalled the fears which had
harassed him in the morning, and felt that God in
his providence had met his case, and scattered
these fears. He resolved to learn from this incident one lesson, — worth many hundreds to him, —
to do present duty, and trust the morrow with God.

Of all the gifts which a generous people can
bring to their pastor, it is seldom that any is quite
as much to *their* purpose as money. That will
go, as they wish it to go, just where it is most
needed; Mr. Holbrook found it so in the present
instance. It paid his debts, — and thus it made
him and Lucy cheerful again; it added a better
than golden link to that chain which was fast
binding him to his people. He returned to his
study, with fresh courage and hope.

Lucy determined to take warning by this occurrence. She very well knew that their friends
could not be expected to come forward thus gen-

erously to help them out of every emergency; and she secretly resolved, she would endeavor to bring their expenses within their income. With much resolution, she set about her economical plans. She had fewer lamps filled, and less cake made; she sometimes went without the pudding, for which she must buy milk and eggs. She cooked soup for her dinners more frequently than before, and closed her purse against the thousand little nicknacks which tempt one to spend money thoughtlessly in a city. But let her economize as she would, it seemed as if something always happened to use up all she saved. Her own health being still delicate, her physician insisted upon her riding occasionally; and every ride of an hour cost her a dollar, and this would have gone far in milk and eggs. In order, therefore, to meet her riding bills, she resorted to the device of giving up her nursery fire. A bed was to be moved into the study, which was always warm, and during the day, the baby was to be kept in the back parlor.

Mr. Holbrook bore this innovation manfully one week; but the charm of his study was broken. It was no longer a place sacred from intrusion; Bridget's knock, or Lucy's more quiet entrance, broke in upon and entangled many a struggling train of thought.

On one Saturday morning, when each minute was precious to him, for his sermon was but half done, the door bell rung repeatedly, and many ladies called. Miss Tot woke up suddenly, much out of humor, and would have no voice but hers heard. The young mother, looking pale and anxious, endeavored to hush her, and also carry on conversation with her guests, but it was all in vain; so Bridget was summoned, and the crying child sent to the study. As ladies continued to call, she made a longer visit there than was desirable, considering the circumstances of the case. Mr. Holbrook's "application," chiming as it must with Bridget's hushing and baby's crying, was likely to be a notable specimen of discordant pathos.

The precious Saturday morning was wholly lost, and the clock struck two that night on the old church tower, before the young minister could drop his pen, and lay his weary head upon his pillow. It can scarcely be said that he slept, for his mind worked on with the "application," until broad daylight, — and then he rose for his Sabbath day's work. Well was it for him, that he was yet young and strong.

"Lucy," said he, at breakfast on Monday morning, "we must move back into the nursery to-day. I must have a study, — we will retrench somewhere else."

11*

"Yes," said Lucy, "we will. I cannot make a nursery of the parlor, and I do not wish to try any longer."

Lucy, as she gained strength, took the air by walking rather than riding, though contrary to her physician's advice; but the riding bills were too heavy for them. One pleasant morning, she called Bridget away from her work, that she might carry the baby, to make a call with her upon Mrs. Talbot. Mrs. Talbot made much of the little stranger; and Lucy sat down, and very soon was, as usual, giving Mrs. Talbot a sketch of their domestic affairs. She told her how they had incurred a debt; of the opportune present from the people, and of their subsequent attempts to economize. Mrs. Talbot gave Lucy excellent advice on this subject; for, notwithstanding her wealth, she thoroughly understood domestic economy as a system. She had luncheon ordered, and, finally, called John and his shining horses, and sent her visitors home.

After this, John very frequently reined up before " Number Five," and Mrs. Talbot kindly insisted that Lucy and her baby should take an airing. It was always John's business to take the little bundle from the mother in his brawny arms, and it seemed to nestle down in his shaggy coat-sleeves, as if it liked its quarters well; and if a bit of the blanket blew up, John laughed at the plump little face there hidden, and would be sure to hold it so that Mrs. Talbot could see, and she, too, would laugh and be pleased. God bless her for her kindness to that young mother and child. Well is it for this poor world, when to such a heart and hand wealth is given. Thanks, then, to her, and to John and his horses, the little one thrived, and the mother grew strong again.

That same lady, "in our city," who perchance by this time has cut out the collars, rides every day alone in her elegant carriage; and she is very glad when the round has been taken, and the horses heads are turned homeward. She would find that ride a very different thing, if she had each day some delicate one with her, to whom the airing was healing medicine. The increased pleasure such an arrangement would give her, would more than repay the trouble of finding out the number of the dwelling where the delicate one pines.

One of the results of Mrs. Talbot's kindness was, that Lucy became so strong that she was able to bear another reckoning day. She accordingly sat down cheerfully with Mr. Holbrook to cast up accounts. But no casting would bring them out to the satisfaction of the reckoners. It was a fact they had, some how, run behindhand again a little, not much, but just enough to use up all the money which Mr. Holbrook had resolutely put away for the purchase of books, together with a small sum which Lucy had reserved to purchase furs.

"What *shall* I do?" said Mr. Holbrook, "I must have the books, come what will of it. I need now more than a hundred dollars' worth."

"What shall we do?" said Lucy; "suppose we give up our parlor fire."

Mr. Holbrook laughed at Lucy's economical plans. "We must sooner give up a thousand and one little things," said he.

"What little things?" asked Lucy.

"I can hardly tell myself, but more money than we think for slips away on what seems to be trifles. One is constantly tempted to buy in a city."

"I know that," said Lucy, "and I have been trying to retrench there. Now we know precisely what our living expenses are, suppose we estimate these nicknacks, and see what we can spare for them. Then I will put by just so much every week, and we will make a rule that we will not spend a penny more. See here," said she, opening a fancy writing-desk and lifting a little slide, "here is a nice corner all lined with blue silk, made on purpose to keep it in. You put the money there every Monday morning, will you?"

"What difference will it make," said he, laughing, "whether it is there or in my pocket, if we limit ourselves as to the amount? Is not one dollar as good as another?"

"No," said Lucy, "if I can come and see — there, there is just so much I can have to spend and no more, I can manage it better."

"Well," said Mr. Holbrook, "a woman has a way of her own of managing the finances, I see; you shall do as you like."

A small sum for incidental expenses was placed in the blue corner, and Lucy began on her new plan. She was soon astonished by the amount of money which slipped away on trifles. It seemed to her as if she could not fold her hands without paying a sixpence for the privilege.

CHAPTER XV.

ECONOMY.

By good management and good resolution, Lucy
succeeded for a time in keeping within the limits
prescribed for her incidental expenses, but now
other demands were made upon the purse; for
when she was again able to visit among their
people, a servant was needed to take care of the
baby. Mr. Holbrook was obliged to go to remote
Intelligence Offices before a suitable one could be
found. This cost him time, and when accomplished, still another necessity for expense arose.
Lucy had overestimated her strength; she was
unable to walk as she had once done, and was
often obliged to ride in an omnibus. Now no
riding could be cheaper than this, certainly; she
could go from one end of the city to another for a
sixpence. On this account, Mr. and Mrs. Holbrook
patronized the omnibuses liberally, and, by Friday
night, every penny of Lucy's hoard for that week,
had gone for " tickets!"

So Lucy stood, holding the slide to the empty
blue corner, and laughing heartily at her discov-

ery. " We cannot afford to ride even in an omnibus," said she.

" What can you do, then," said Mr. Holbrook,
" you are not able to walk ? "

" I must give up making calls, for as Mrs. Talbot says, I am not called upon to do more than I
can do."

" I ride," said Mr. Holbrook, "to save time ; it
is worth more than a sixpence to me."

" Suppose we put by a dollar a week more
for tickets," said Lucy, "if we must — we must,
that 's all."

Mr. Holbrook hesitated. Another servant had
been hired, and many books were needed, and a
new Review had just been subscribed for. No
satisfactory arrangement could be made, and the
matter was left as it stood. After this, Lucy rode
less and called less ; she was learning to count her
sixpences.

About this time Lucy received a letter from
her old friend, Mary Jay, who communicated the
news that she was about changing her name into
that of Mary Day, and hoped to make a bridal
visit to the city. Mr. Holbrook and Lucy remembered how gratifying had been the attentions
shown them on their bridal tour, and they wished
to do everything in their power to make such a
visit pleasant to their friends.

Mrs. Kennedy happened in the day before the

expected guests were to arrive, and found Lucy making preparations to receive them.

"Cannot I help you any?" she asked.

"I should like to have you show me how to put up these curtains," said Lucy, as she led the way to the guest-chamber, which was a pleasant room directly over the study, and commanding the same western view.

"Is there covering enough on the bed?" she inquired.

"I should think so," said Mrs. Kennedy, laughing, "one — two — three cotton spreads."

Lucy dropped the end of the curtain and looked up, with a blush on her cheek. Her house-keeper's pride was slightly mortified; in a moment, however, she merrily laughed it off.

"No, I have not bought my blankets yet," said she, "one of these days, when our ship comes in, I am going to have them."

"There is no hurry about it," said Mrs. Kennedy.

"So I think," said Lucy, "I should not take any comfort in buying my blankets, and feeling that Mr. Holbrook had to go without books."

At tea time, Bridget entered the dining-room with a bundle almost as large as herself. It contained the much wished for blankets; they had been sent, "with Mrs. Kennedy's love."

Mary Day and her husband arrived on the

day appointed. The two old school-mates met again with sincere pleasure, yet neither found the other precisely what she left her. Much of their girlish glee had vanished with the years, and Lucy, with that image of herself in her arms, had lost all appearance of the school girl. As for Mary, she being just married, it was quite reasonable and proper that her eye should continually seek him who occupied all her thoughts. The two friends had not, therefore, such earnest chats together as they used to have over the old headboard in the boarding-house.

Lucy was very anxious to make their visit pleasant, and she was mindful of Bridget that she should do her best, and Mr. Holbrook also devoted all the time he could spare to his guests. "Be given to hospitality," was an injunction of Scripture which he delighted to obey. Thus all things contributed to give Mr. and Mrs. Day, as they said, "a charming visit."

After their departure, Lucy, needing some 'change,' lifted the blue slide. Lo! the corner was empty, — all had gone on the bridal visit.

"There," said she, "when we set aside this sum we never thought to allow for company. How our money goes."

"Never mind, this time," said Mr. Holbrook, "brides do not visit us every day."

Lucy soon began to think, that if brides did not, some one else did, every day. The company career commenced. One visitor prepared the way for another, and the minister and his wife were seldom alone. Many who came to " Number Five" were country friends, to whom the city was entirely new. Neither Mr. nor Mrs. Holbrook felt that they could let them come and go, and yet pay them no special attention. There was aunt Nancy, and cousin Peggy, and uncle Ralph, — why, they visited a city but once or twice in a life-time. They must be taken to see the ' lions,' or they would scarcely feel repaid for the trouble of coming. Thus, on only the common courtesies which one feels compelled to offer in the city, Lucy's cornered hoard many and many a time slipped away.

Then there were the relations at home. Little Johnny must have a rattle sent him by the minister, and Sarah must have a doll, and the little cousins over the way must not be forgotten ; a package of confectionary, a book, a toy, or a ribbon, must be sent to them. These trifling presents which seemed so little singly, in the aggregate, frequently drained the blue corner. Yet what was a shilling spent on a baby's rattle? Nothing, — and yet the minister's salary was made up of shillings, and they were not so many as to be innumerable

One day Lucy, as was her frequent experience, went seeking change, and found none.

"There," said she, emphatically, closing the slide, "I have about made up my mind that we are too poor to spend sixpences. We cannot afford to spend anything less than a dollar."

Mr. Holbrook was sometimes troubled by this. He felt unwilling to be cramped in exercising hospitality, and yet more money was slipping through their fingers than they had to spare, and the library shelves were yet empty. But this fact had no influence upon their company, for still they came, and neither Mr. Holbrook nor Lucy wished it otherwise. Mr. Holbrook knew that if he lived in the city, he must keep an open house.

"Come what will of it," said he to Lucy, "we must be hospitable."

"What *shall* we economize in?" said Lucy, laughing. "Everything we try turns out just so. After awhile, you say, 'Come what will of it, we must have this.'"

"I do not know," said Mr. Holbrook, "unless we can economize more on our table. We can have good food, and a plenty of it; but let it be simple and unexpensive."

"Something might be saved," said Lucy, "if you would do the marketing. I cannot get out with a baby; I have to send Bridget almost every day, and she has not much discretion."

"I will do the marketing," said the minister, "it will be a saving; I will begin to-day."

He opened the door to go immediately out, and found Mr. Thornburn standing on the steps, with a fish in his hand.

"I was buying our dinner," said he, "and these fish come in so fresh and nice, I thought my minister might like a bite, and so I brought one along."

"We are very much obliged to you," said Lucy, showing her pleasant face at the door; "you must step in a minute, if it is only to look at the baby. Are you well, at home?"

"Yes," said Mr. Thornburn, carefully wiping his feet before he entered, "all well, I thank you."

He sat down, played with the baby, had a pleasant chat with his minister and wife, and went away even better pleased than before, at the opportunity of doing a kindness to his minister.

"Now, Charles," said Lucy, with sparkling eyes, and holding up the fish, "how nice this is; it has just saved us what we overran in our allowance last week. What use is there in troubling about living? When the pinch comes, we are always provided for."

"Yes," said Mr. Holbrook; "but then this is aid which we cannot calculate upon. It is not often we receive a present which saves us money. We live better than we should, if our people gave us nothing; they add much to the comforts and conveniences around us; but their presents do not always diminish the actual expenses of living. If they did not send us such things, we should go without them."

"It is so," said Lucy; "we have them to thank for many comforts; but frequently I think they overestimate the help which their presents really give us."

"Yes, — still, it is just as generous in them to remember us so often; and with good management, Lucy, we shall not run over this quarter, I think."

"With your good marketing, you mean," said Lucy, slyly.

"Why, do not I mean to do it?"

"Certainly, you have the best intentions in the world; but I wonder how many mornings I shall hear Bridget rapping at the study door, 'Please, sir, no meat in the house for dinner.'"

"You will see."

"And Saturday nights, when the sermons press, what will become of the marketing then?"

"I intend to make a business of it," was the reply.

Notwithstanding the minister's efforts, the market frequently closed on Saturday night, and the Sunday's dinner, — was not. This was the case, on one occasion, when the Rev. Mr. Sheply came in late to spend the Sabbath with his friends at "Number Five." Lucy, knowing by the hour that it was hopeless to make preparation then, said nothing about it.

The next morning, immediately after breakfast, Bridget came to her ; " What shall I get for dinner, ma'am ? "

" Ham and eggs, — there is nothing else."

" O, indeed, ma'am ! the ham is all gone but one slice, and there aint but three eggs left in the house."

" Dear me ! " said Mrs. Holbrook, " what shall I do ? I was depending upon that. Well, there is no way but to make the best of what we have."

At noon, just as they were to sit down to dinner, Bridget opened the parlor door, just wide enough to show a red face ; " Please, ma'am, step here," said she.

Mrs. Holbrook went out immediately. There was Bridget, with the poor little slice of ham burned to a cinder, and two eggs in a saucer.

" The fat, ma'am," said she, " caught a-fire, and I went to put it out, and dropped the poker on the egg and broke it."

Lucy's dinner thus served, and Bridget's countenance, as she displayed it, presented such a comical sight, that Lucy could not refrain from laughing.

"Well," said she, as soon as she could speak, "we must dispense with the ham and eggs to-day, certainly. Make a good cup of coffee, and give us bread and butter and pie. And next week, Bridget, you or I will remember the marketing."

"That, indade, we will, ma'am," said Bridget.

The dinner, such as it was, came up, — and all were seated at the table. After the blessing was asked, Mr. Holbrook appeared to be waiting for something. He was always particular to set meat before those who were to preach, knowing that ministers frequently suffered from want of it.

Lucy, in endeavoring to apologize for her dinner, began to laugh again, and, finally, felt called upon to explain their marketing arrangements. Mr. Sheply fully appreciated the exigencies which will arise in a minister's family. Fortunately, also, he could drink coffee, and, seeing that the lady of the house retained her good humor, the dinner, or lunch rather, passed off well.

On Monday morning, Mr. Holbrook spoke of it to Lucy. Said he, "it never will answer for us to be without a dinner in the house. We are liable to visitors at all hours, and our table must be such that we shall be willing to ask a friend to sit down to it. Economy beyond a certain point is inappropriate."

"Just so," said Lucy, "we must set a comfortable table. Where then *shall* we economize?"

"We must live," was the reply.

"And let the books go?"

"O, those books," said the minister, with a sigh; "I have almost made up my mind to run in debt for them."

CHAPTER XVI.

CHARITY.

BEFORE long, his mind was fully made up; the books were ordered, and placed in the study. Their presence cheered and encouraged the minister, and he went to work with increased zest, as we do when friends are by. Every fragment of time was carefully hoarded, and every unimportant miscellaneous duty cut off, that he might devote himself more to his books.

Lucy wished to promote this object as much as she could. She generously assumed almost the entire burden of house-keeping. She troubled her husband for nothing which could be avoided. In addition to this, she received and entertained all the company, of which there was a constant flow, and also made calls when it was practicable. When it is remembered, that she was both a young mother and a young house-keeper; that the excitement of a city life was entirely new to her, it will not be wondered at, that such a pressure from all sides, sometimes proved too much for her young strength, and that, when the warm days came on, she be-

came debilitated. Her appetite, and what was of
more value, her good spirits, failed her. What-
ever she did, cost much effort. The baby grew
heavy in her arms; the journey to the kitchen
became so formidable, that she was frequently
induced to let things go, rather than look after
them. Mr. Holbrook observed with pain her daily
increasing feebleness, and often left his study that
he might relieve her of some domestic care.   On
one occasion, in particular, he was going down
town, and her pale face seemed to follow him.
He remembered how poor her appetite had been
for some time, and, as he was thinking of it, his
eye caught sight of some fine grapes in a window.
He immediately went in and inquired the price;
it was exorbitant, — he hesitated, but the pale
face still looked at him, and he bought. Taking
them carefully in a paper, he went on his walk,
and soon saw an advertisement of a new commentary, — one for which he had been anxiously waiting. He stepped into the book-store; this also
was expensive, but he must have it, and again he
bought. When, on his return, Lucy sat by his
side, eating the grapes with relish, and looking at
the new book with pleasure; — she resolved not
to ask, " what was the *cost?* " but, for once, she
would feel rich, and, by and by, when she grew
stronger, make up for it by extra economy. Before

this "by and by" came, — a poor woman called
at "Number Five," and found Mr. Holbrook alone
in the parlor. She told him her story, which he
heard with much interest, and then went to beg
Lucy to see her.

"Why should I go," said Lucy, hesitatingly; "I
cannot help her any. I have given away now
everything I can spare, and more too. Scarcely
a day passes without some call for money or old
clothes."

"Yes, I know it," said Mr, Holbrook; "still I
think you had better go down."

Lucy went, reluctantly, to hear a tale of woe
which she felt she could not relieve. The poor
woman was sitting in a corner; a child stood by
her with a handkerchief tied over her head.

The story was briefly this: the woman was an
American, and her husband, a slater by trade,
had, the week before, been instantly killed by a
fall from a scaffold. She and six children were left
destitute. She wished to obtain money enough
to return with her children to her friends in a
distant State, and to do so before the birth of the
seventh, which was soon expected. The minister,
whose church she had attended, advised her to
seek aid from the clergymen. "So I've come,"
said she to Mrs. Holbrook. "Your husband asked
me if I had a character; — I ha'n't, for I did not

know as I must bring a character; I never begged before."

The tears rolled down her cheeks as she said this, her tone was mournful, and the child looked up as if she had more than a child's share of grief, — as if she bore her own and her mother's also. Lucy's sympathies were at once excited, and before long, she was opening the study door.

" Charles," said she, " I do feel sorry for her; cannot we afford to help her a little?"

" Yes," was his ready reply, and his money was equally ready. To this Lucy added a hood and shawl of her own, which she tied over the little girl, — she could not send her away naked.

"I shall not make up my extra economy this week," thought Lucy, as she slowly returned to the nursery. "I should have, though, if it had not been for this poor woman. But then how could we help giving? There is such a comfort, too, in giving. Well, there are more weeks to come, — I'll try again."

Another week, bringing its busy round of care and duty, was welcomed by Lucy with this wholesome resolution — to *save* that she might compensate for some luxuries indulged in in her illness, but before it closed, another applicant for money made his call at " Number Five." He was a colored minister, begging for his poor and struggling church.

This was a call to which nearly all the clergymen in the city had responded, and Mr. Holbrook felt that he must give; and accordingly he gave.

When he told Lucy, she appeared to be in a brown study about it.

" I am glad you gave," said she, at length, if you can afford it.

" I cannot afford it," said he, " but I do not know how to economize in this thing. Situated as we pastors in a city are, we must give often, whether we are able to do it or not.

" Please announce the thing in which we *can* economize when you have found it, will you?" said Lucy, laughing, " that will be a marvellous discovery."

" We must live," was, as usual, the minister's reply.

On this conclusion he quietly rested until reckoning day, — then, after looking over his bills, he was ready to add to it these three words — *on our salary;* for again they had run behindhand, not much, it is true, but just enough to prevent his advancing even a five dollar bill towards the debt at the book-store. Still as the past quarter was the most expensive in the year, he was not without hope that by the close of another, they should make some advance. In order to accomplish this, it seemed absolutely necessary that they should

13

limit themselves in giving, and that their various objects of charity should be well defined. Many cases of distress came to their knowledge which they could not relieve by money; they sought to do it by personal attention and efforts to obtain employment for the needy, and, of course, the labor of this system of benevolence fell mostly upon Lucy. She made many journies from one end of the city to another, which used her time, strength, and omnibus tickets, and not unfrequently she found she had been sent on a " fool's errand."

When she was once telling Mrs. Kennedy of some case of disappointment and vexation, she said to her ; " you will get imposed upon, Mrs. Holbrook, if you believe all that the beggars tell you. I have learned not to pay much heed to those who beg at the door. We have so many societies now for relieving the poor, that those who go about so, are usually idle and worthless, and will not take up any trade but begging. We have as many worthy objects as we can aid ; but it takes strangers I find, a long while to learn this."

This remark induced Lucy to make inquiries of Bridget respecting a woman who came regularly every week to " Number Five," for broken pieces.

" She tells me," said Bridget, " that she has a great family of little children, and can't get work, and she should certainly starve if 't was n't for what we gave her."

" Do you know where she lives ? "

" Yes, ma'am, she told me to-day."

" I wish you would put your things on, and go and make some inquiries about her."

Bridget went, and soon returned much excited. " I found the place," she said, " but the plague of a thief has n't a child in the world, — nothing at all, ma'am, but a house full of boarders, which she is a feeding out of *us* — the vile crathur."

" Do not let her come in again," said Mrs. Holbrook, " and Bridget, you need not give away any more broken pieces, until I tell you to do so. We will find some other way of disposing of them." There was now more prospect that Lucy's *saving* plan would be successful, for she was learning some of the traps which prove a snare to most young city housekeepers ; but particularly so to ministers' wives, since it is expected that they should abound in " whatsoever things are of good report."

Experience, certainly, was teaching both the minister and his wife the cost of living, and yet one problem remained unsolved ; " how to make the two ends meet." Their salary was amply sufficient for their support, or ought to be, and at first they could not understand what consumed it. After a time, they learned to make allowance for a variety of uncalculated expenses, which are indispensable to the position of a city pastor. It

was not, therefore, so much the cost of living, as
the cost of the *profession* which embarrassed
them; in any other position, they could have
lived comfortably on a less sum. This *cost of the
profession* was a secret which they did not at first
understand, and which many of their people have
not learned to this day. They know nothing, in
fact, of the tools which their minister needs, and
they take but little pains to inform themselves.
What the merchant, the carpenter, the baker
must have, they can tell you readily, if you inquire, and give you the amount of capital necessary for the prosecution of their business; but
when it comes to the minister, — O! all *he* needs
is the Bible; having this, what should he ask
more? Therefore, when they sit down to reckon
up what their pastor must have to live upon, books,
newspapers, and periodicals are left quite out of
the reckoning; these ought not to be considered
necessary expenses; he must make a shift to do
without them.

Said a learned and highly honored judge, whose
liberal education induced some applicants to call
upon him to assist in furnishing a library for their
pastor, said he, gravely, as if delivering an opinion
from the bench : " *It does not require many books
to convert souls !* "

Another important item is also left out in the

estimate. It is the cost of keeping the preacher
himself in repair. An occupation which consumes
not only time and strength, but which makes heavy
drafts on mind and heart; which presses on the
conscience until it secures a most unreserved self-
devotion, is beyond their comprehension. It wears
out the mortal frame faster than they imagine.
They acknowledge that their minister works-hard,
and lives fast, but *they* also work hard. Why
should he need money for recreation and journies?
They never throw away a dollar for such a purpose. No, and never need to do it. Rest and
recreation are not of vital importance to them, —
it is to him. Something more than sleep is needed
to recruit the wearied brain.

More from ignorance, therefore, than from any
want of generosity, many of the Downs Street
people rested on the conviction that Mr. Holbrook's salary was ample enough to ensure his
"living easy." They, with their great families,
had not much more; some of them not so much.
In making provision for him, they had never
reckoned the capital which his profession demanded. It is not, therefore, to be wondered at,
that at the close of the year, between the two
ends, a debt lay, — a debt for books.

CHAPTER XVII.

THE MINISTERS' WIVES.

An invitation for an evening party was left at
" Number Five." Mr. Holbrook, hearing of it,
said, " It would be quite impossible for him to go,
for it was to be on the evening of his weekly
lecture." Lucy did not much regret this, for she
had learned to value quiet, and to sit by her cradle
in the nursery, with her work, and have the minister read for an evening, was more attractive
to her than going out. She, therefore, readily fell
in with his decision. In the course of the day,
Mr. Holbrook heard that most of the ministers in
the city had been invited, and he concluded to go.

He was writing busily in his study, when the
tea bell rang. His cup of tea coolly waited for him
until seven, when, in reward for its courtesy, he
swallowed it hastily, and hastened to his vestry.
After meeting, his deacons stopped him on business, and it was even later than usual when he
returned. He was weary, and would gladly have
gone to rest rather than to a party; but as he
found Lucy dressed and waiting for him, he said

nothing of his fatigue, but immediately went out with her.

As they closed the door of their house, the evening air felt chilly and damp.

" I hope we have not far to go," said Lucy, shivering.

" It will be a long walk for you ; had not I better call a carriage ? "

Lucy hesitated a moment. She was already weary, for her baby had been troublesome, and she had had company all day ; it would have been a great comfort to ride, yet she hesitated only for a moment; she had discovered that they could economize in carriage hire.

" No, I thank you," she soon replied, " I can walk." Mr. Holbrook wished, just then, that he was rich.

When they reached the place of their destination, Lucy went up stairs, and as she was laying off her things, she observed a lady looking at her very earnestly. She soon spoke, introduced herself as Mrs. Jay, and apologized for not having immediately recognized Mrs. Holbrook.

" We meet so seldom," said she, pleasantly, " that it is no wonder we forget each other."

When Mr. and Mrs. Holbrook entered the parlor, they found themselves among strangers. Lucy, after a time, stole quietly into a corner, and looked out, in the vain hope of seeing some of the Downs Street people ; but none were visible, and she was made sensible, by a certain homesickness of heart, that love had sprung up between her and them. By and by Mrs. Lacy came and spoke kindly, though in a patronizing manner to her, and she still found Lucy shy. In the ebbing and flowing of the crowd, several ministers' wives were, at one time, left standing near her. They all expressed regret that they should not oftener meet each other.

Said one, " Why cannot we have a regular time for meeting, as our husbands do ? I think it would be profitable to all of us."

" Yes, it would," said another, " but the diffi-culty would be in making it out. We have all of us so much to do at home and in our parishes, I fancy we gladly dispense with any visits which are not absolutely necessary."

" If we were as smart as Mrs. D.," said another, " we could accomplish it."

" What did she do, that was remarkable ?"

" She made it a rule to call three times a year on every individual in their society."

" Indeed ! she had no children, I suppose."

" Yes, she had six."

" She must be a very remarkable woman; I should like to see her."

" She is dead."

"I should suppose so," said one of the group, speaking briskly ; "ministers' wives cannot do so much more than every body else, without paying for it."

The plan of a regular meeting for ministers' wives was dropped.

When Mr. and Mrs. Holbrook started to go home, they found it raining hard. Lucy was not prepared for so violent a storm, and was, therefore, obliged to ride.

"Have you enjoyed yourself this evening?" inquired Lucy of Mr. Holbrook, as they were riding home.

"Yes, pretty well, only I missed my people."

"So did I," said Lucy.

The minister, as time passed, said, with increased emphasis and feeling, — "*my people.*" This growing attachment made inroads on his schemes of study ; it tempted him to think much of their wants, and little of his own.

When Mr. Holbrook was on his way to market next morning, he met Mr. Kennedy. Mr. Kennedy had been purchasing gloves for himself, and finding a lot which was unusually good, he had also taken a pair for his minister, which he now handed to him. When Lucy saw them, her face was bright with smiles.

"How fortunate," said she, "they are just what

you needed, and must have bought.   This present has saved you all that money, and that will more than make up for our carriage hire last night."

"That carriage hire seems to trouble your conscience, Lucy; you are becoming as calculating as a Yankee."

"Somebody must calculate," was her reply, "if we are to live in the city on our salary."

CHAPTER XVIII.

LATITUDE AND LONGITUDE.

THIS matter of *living,* soon gave Mr. Holbrook less and less anxiety. In the way of economizing, he did all which he thought he could with propriety do, and when necessity demanded some extra outlay, he could not but observe, that something usually turned up to make amends for it; for instance, as Lucy would have said, "Mr. Kennedy's gloves and the carriage hire." One thing was so frequently set over against another, that Lucy became convinced, that this order was a settled arrangement of Providence for their support. Had not the Downs Street people been to the full as generous and thoughtful as they were, their pastor would have had no means of meeting those wants which they could not appreciate. True, the pecuniary value of their gifts to him was much less than they sometimes supposed, and yet they added so many little comforts to living, that he was able to dispense with many things which, under other circumstances, would have been necessary, and the money was appropriated to profes-

sional "capital." True, it would have been much
to the young minister's mind, if by hiring service
he could have bought his time as well as library,
but to have secured this needed at least double
his salary, — which was a consummation, however
devoutly wished, scarcely to be hoped for.

Mr. Holbrook, the more he was enabled to throw
off pecuniary care, became more devoted to his
great work, and the minor matters of living dwin-
dled in importance. He gave himself little anxiety
about his debts ; not even the accumulating one at
the book-store. Well was it, that in proportion
as he relinquished this care, Lucy took it. She
became more and more prudent and economical,
and this was the reason why the gulf between
the two ends did not widen much.

But Mr. Holbrook did not escape trials, for time
brought him into those of a different character
from any which he had heretofore experienced.
He began to obtain an insight into the machinery
of city churches, and the relative position of his
own church.

The Downs Street Church, like all the others
which were not within a certain geographical circle,
was compelled to struggle for its foothold. It suffered for want of a nucleus which it could not
command. There is a law of attraction stronger
than that of gravitation, which draws city people

towards certain charmed districts. Here it is an
" up-town" district, — there it is a " central " district, — and elsewhere it is a " west-end." A
church beyond the magic limits, is like a shop on
the unfashionable side of Broadway. People will
go to the fashionable street to hear preaching, as
they will to buy their silks and broadcloths. They
will go out of their way, and pass and re-pass every
Sabbath the door of some feeble, struggling church.
Here they are needed, — here they would be welcomed, — here their presence would cheer and encourage a drooping band of Christ's devoted fol-
lowers, — but on they go.

" Stop, my friend, ought not this church which
you are leaving behind, to be sustained?"

" Most certainly it is every way desirable. We
must have a church here for the common people.
They will run in when one is handy, — and there
are enough of them hereabouts, — they ought to
be thankful that so good provision is made for
them."

" But why do *you* pass on? — you are bound
on a long walk; this church is as handy for you
as for your neighbors."

" *I*? O, *I* — *I*, have always been to Dr. Jay's, —
and my wife is acquainted there, and *we* could n't
think of coming *here*." He buttons up his coat,
and bows with cool politeness, as if he thought

14

your questions impertinent. *He* is not one of the *common* people he would have you know, — on he goes, enters Dr. Jay's church, takes his old seat, and is lost in the crowd. There is a little verse in a certain old book which tells about " hiding one's talent in a napkin," — our friend might think of with profit as he returns home; but if he would avoid a *personal* application of it, he should also avoid passing that struggling church which he acknowledges " *must be sustained.*" If he wishes to profit by it, let him pause on the threshold of the humbler church, and ask himself, " Am I needed at Dr. Jay's? — Am I not needed here?" and then let conscience settle the questions.

On a pleasant Sabbath, so many people passed the Downs Street Church on their way up town, that the labor of sustaining it was great for its pastor. He was expected not only to fill his church, but by some magic to bring it up abreast with the others; for many of his people had no idea of the geographical difficulties which stood in the way. Competition — competition, — this was the silent watchword. Mr. Holbrook resolutely shut his ears to it; it injured the purity of his purposes, — he turned away from it, for he wished to keep his " eye single " to the great object of preaching. He needed to struggle against it, for he encountered it everywhere, and, for the most part, he did succeed in disengaging himself from this snare, and in preaching the truth with enthusiasm for its own sake. Yet this again, in his early ministry, was a source of trial to him; it led him to come looking "for fruit, when, as yet, there was none." Not unfrequently this disappointment made him unhappy. Had he not been settled for so long a time, — and what were the results? What good had been done by his preaching?

When depressed from this cause, Mr. Holbrook found it difficult to keep faithfully and steadily at his work. He sighed for the encouragement of success ; he felt that it was time to expect that. He was a young laborer, and had not yet learned to calculate " seed-time and harvest."

When these clouds were in the sky, Lucy went among the people and set " traps to catch sunbeams." She carefully gathered, in her calls, all that was cheering, and treasured up little expressions of interest and attachment for the pastor, and brought them home to silver the clouds.

When thus disheartened, the city pastor was made sensitive to various other trials which were inseparable from his position.

One afternoon, he returned from a meeting of the ministers, but instead of going to his study, he went to the nursery, and sat down there in silence.

" Anything trouble you this afternoon?" inquired Lucy.

" No, — not particularly ; but I find I make slow progress in becoming acquainted with the ministers here. I stand just about where I did when I first came."

" Is it their fault or yours ? "

" Neither, I am inclined to think, but the natural consequence of their great pressure of professional duty. They are so much crowded by their work, they have but very little time for social inter-course, and a young minister is necessarily left to make his way alone. On this account, I believe his probation is much more severe in the city than in the country. He must, for the most part, force his way unaided, and as long as there is so much to be done in our city churches, I do not see any help for it. The difficulty lies, not in want of dis-position on their part, but in want of time."

" Do you need more social intercourse with them ? "

" Yes, sometimes I do feel the want of sym-pathy and companionship ; but I comfort myself with the hope, that more of it will come in time."

" Are not you on good terms with any of them ? "

" On good terms, — yes, with all of them ; they all treat me with kindness and courtesy when we do meet, and Dr. Jay does a great deal more than that."

" What does he do ? "

"In the benevolence of his heart, he — pat — ronizes — me."

"Well, what of it," said Lucy, laughing; "do n't you like to be *patronized*?"

"I appreciate his motives," said Mr. Holbrook, slowly, "and feel obliged to him for his good intentions, but a man likes to stand on his own feet."

"Perhaps it is his way of showing you a kindness," said Lucy.

"I understand all that, and yet sometimes, with the very best intentions, mistakes are made on this point. Now, as an example, let me tell you of a little thing which occurred this afternoon. As Dr. Jay and I were walking home together, we were speaking of some preacher, — and Dr. Jay, to wind off with, very obligingly gave me a plan for a sermon."

"It was a good one, I dare say," said Lucy, roguishly.

"Y—e—s," said Mr. Holbrook.

"Will it be of any service to you?"

"I can use it if I should ever be in want of a plan, and could not make one," said Mr. Holbrook.

"But was n't it better than yours are?" persisted Lucy.

She persisted in vain, — no reply did she get, excepting a gleam of mirthfulness, which shot from Mr. Holbrook's eyes, as he raised them to hers.

14*

Silently he went out, and returned to his pleasant green study. He sat down by the window, and looking steadily at the old church tower, he fell into a reverie. His early professional life had its trials ; his church was disadvantageously situated ; his preaching seemed like throwing seed on stony ground ; he had his way to make, it might almost be said, single-handed. Whether he was to be successful or not, the future alone could determine, for in the present there was but little to encourage him.

But this was looking only at the dark side. He turned away from it ; met and grappled with his discouragements as a Christian should, and grew stronger in the combat, as a Christian must. He no longer indulged in reverie, but sat down at his table, and went resolutely to work at his sermon. He would " leave the things which were behind, and press towards the mark."

On the following Sabbath he was rewarded for this faithful effort, for his people listened to his preaching with the greatest interest. Before tea, Mrs. Bent came in to borrow the sermon, that she might read it to her mother ; and she said so much in its praise, that after the door had closed upon her, Lucy could not forbear asking, " If the sermon was not almost as good as it would have been had it been written on Dr. Jay's plan ? " To which saucy question she, very properly, received no reply.

CHAPTER XIX.

DR. DODD.

ONE Monday morning Mr. Holbrook found himself unusually exhausted, for he had preached three times on the preceding Sabbath. Most of the Downs Street people commenced their week's work rested and refreshed; but this was not the case with their minister. He entered on the duties of a busy week, weary. On the next Sabbath, it would be his turn to take charge of the 'United Lecture;' he was expecting to have a meeting on Thursday, a preparatory lecture on Friday, and on Wednesday the Sewing Society met. In addition to this, several cases of illness required his attention.

He walked to the 'West End,' to negotiate an exchange, and was successful. Much relieved by this, he went bravely to work to prepare for his other duties. On Tuesday, he was called to attend two funerals; so that day was broken up. On Thursday, he was called to attend a third funeral, and on Friday, a poor man came requesting him to perform the same sad service, for the fourth time. The man being a stranger, Mr. Holbrook told him, " it was impossible for him to go."

The applicant made no reply to this, but stood silent and sorrowful at the door.

" I think the Rev. Mr. —— will go," continued Mr. Holbrook, " he lives near you."

" I have been to him, and he could n't."

" Where do you attend church ? "

" Nowhere."

" Where did your wife go, when she was living ? "

" Nowhere."

" You had better ask Dr. H."

" He is n't to home."

The man slowly turned the handle of the door, with a friendless and disconsolate look. He could find no one to bury his dead, and he had no tact at pleading for it. His look, however, plead for him eloquently, and Mr. Holbrook consented to go; and thus, yet another afternoon was broken into fragments.

Upon his entering his vestry that evening, a note was handed him from the 'West End' minister, briefly stating, " That sudden illness would prevent his preaching at all, on the following Sabbath." What was Mr. Holbrook to do? Here it was Friday evening. It was with difficulty that he could keep this disappointment out of his thoughts, during his lecture. After the lecture, Mr. Kennedy stopped to speak with him, and told him that Dr. Dodd was in the city; he came in by the evening boat.

Now Dr. Dodd was an eminent clergyman from a distant city. Mr. Holbrook replied, " that he should be happy to call upon him the next morning, and invite him to preach."

He went, accordingly, at an early hour. After a pleasant social interview with the Doctor, he asked him to preach for him on the following day.

To this proposal, Dr. Dodd did not cordially respond. He had not yet formed his plans, — he 'had run away for a little rest, — he was not sure that it would be wise for him to preach at all;' in short, he ' talked off,' and was entirely non-committal. Mr. Holbrook's sensitive feelings instantly took the alarm. He urged the matter no more. Why should he? The Downs Street church was not an 'important' church. Dr. Dodd might not expect to be asked to go out of his way, to preach to any but an 'important' church. Taking his leave, therefore, Mr. Holbrook hastened home, for the precious Saturday morning was fast slipping away. He was going rapidly up stairs to his study, when Lucy met him.

" Lucy," said he, " do not have me interrupted for anything but a case of life or death, if you can help it."

"Why?" said Lucy.

"Because I must write a sermon before night."

"Was Dr. Dodd already engaged?"

"No."

"Why did n't he preach for you, then?"

"I did not inquire," said Mr. Holbrook, in a tone of some feeling. He passed on, entered his room, and locked the door. Contending emotions roused and disturbed him. It was the first time in his pastoral life that he had come personally in contact with that spirit of poor ambition which sometimes creeps into the hearts, and silently influences the conduct of even good men. He met it now in such a form as to wound him, not so much on his own account, as on account of his people. But just in proportion as they seemed to take a low place in the estimation of others, they rose in his. If they were in danger of being overlooked, it was needful their pastor should see to it that they lacked not for bread. To the " poor was the gospel *once* preached," thought he, as he folded his sermon paper, " and my poor people shall have the best I can give them."

With this determination he sat down late on Saturday morning to prepare his sermon. True, he was exhausted by a week of hard labor, but necessity drove him. He put pen to paper; his subject presented itself; thoughts flowed fast as fingers could write. Lucy delayed dinner, — the minister could not stop to dine. She took his dinner to the study and begged him to eat, — no, he could not stop to eat. She left it and went down troubled.

The tea bell rang, — but the study lamp, already lighted, stood on the study table, and by it sat the minister still writing, — and there was the still untasted dinner. Lucy delayed tea, — he did not come; again she went and begged him, almost with tears in her eyes, to stop and take some refreshment, — he came down for about five minutes, then returned immediately to his study, and locked the door.

The hour hand was fast running on to nine, — Mrs. Holbrook called Bridget.

"Anything for dinner to-morrow, Bridget?"

"Not a grain of meat in the house, ma'am."

"Do run over then to the market before it closes, and, Bridget, be sure and cook some nicely for Mr. Holbrook's breakfast, he has eaten nothing at all to-day."

Bridget did as she was directed. Lucy retired, and was soon asleep. The baby cried, and this woke her, and also called Mr. Holbrook in.

"What time is it?" asked Lucy.

"Just striking two, I believe."

"O do n't sit up any longer, Charles; you will not be able to preach at all if you do."

"I do not intend to sit up longer, — I am through."

The morrow proved what necessity could force from the young preacher. His partial and attentive people considered his sermon very wonderful. They knew nothing of the midnight oil and young strength which had been consumed upon it.

Mr. Kennedy in particular, with his pleased and expressive countenance, attracted Lucy's attention, even before he stopped to shake hands with his minister. The two went down the aisle together, and Lucy being just behind them, overheard Mr. Kennedy say, "Dr. Dodd preached this morning for Dr. Jay, and is to preach for Dr. B. this afternoon." Lucy looked up to her husband, surprised. A gleam of mirth which shot from his averted eyes, let her into a secret which she had not understood the day before.

This forced effort had certainly been a successful one, but a succession of similar efforts, which circumstances seemed to require, left Mr. Holbrook exhausted and depressed, and he found it impossible to get along without frequent exchanges.

This called forth some remarks from Mrs. Bent, who joined Lucy on her walk home one Sabbath.

"Is Mr. Holbrook well to-day?" she inquired.

"Not very," replied Lucy, "he has overworked himself lately."

"I do wish he could always stay in his own pulpit," said Mrs. Bent, trying to smile.

"O, he cannot do that," said Lucy.

"I wish so too," said Mrs. Vinton, who just then joined them, "we do not like to have him exchange. We had rather hear him talk, any time, than hear others preach."

At night, Lucy repeated these remarks to Mr. Holbrook.

"Dr. B.'s people feel just so about him, I presume," was his reply. "I could not get them to listen to me, and some of them were reading hymns while I was preaching."

Lucy felt a little provoked at this. "Our people are not rude, at any rate," said she, "for Dr. B. told me after church, they had given him good attention."

Mr. Holbrook was always pleased when his people were praised; he was fast becoming identified with them. Sometimes he asked himself, if to serve a temporary end, he was not neglecting that culture which would eventually fit him for greater efforts? But then, his work was in his hands, and he must do it, or it must be left undone.

15

CHAPTER XX.

NEW MEASURES.

Mr. Holbrook was called upon to encounter other professional trials, equally unexpected. Among these, was an evening call from several gentlemen, members of his church; deacon Silas, and Messrs. Lovering and Sampson. One after another they dropped in, so nearly together, that their meeting seemed more like design than accident, though they in no way intimated this, but sat down, as if to have a pleasant chat with their minister. Gradually, the conversation turned from general to particular subjects.

"We don't seem to have many applications to our Examining Committee lately," remarked Mr. Sampson; "I don't know how to account for it."

"No, we are falling into a cold state," remarked deacon Silas, solemnly.

"The fact is, brethren, and we may as well out with it," said Mr. Lovering, "we are all asleep; we ought to wake up and do something."

"Yes," said Mr. Sampson, "I've been thinking

it over, and I feel as if we ought to have more
meetings.   Some measures must be taken to
rouse us."

Deacon Silas looked at the minister.   A feeler
had been put forth, and he sought, by a glance of
his keen gray eye, to see how it was received.
The minister was doubtful whether new plans of
effort would accord well with those in which he
was already deeply engaged, but to give his friends
an opportunity to unfold their views, he was silent.

"Why would n't it be a good plan to get up
four days' meetings," said Mr. Lovering, "our
minister could have all the help he wanted, and
they take right smartly in other places.   They
are having revivals and crowded houses, and
everybody gets wide awake wherever they try
such meetings.   Over in D——, now, they are
working wonders."

"Yes," continued deacon Silas, in the solemn
tone characteristic of him, "drops are falling in
other places.   Certainly we must open our windows if we would catch a blessing.   I am not sure
but protracted meetings will be just the thing for
us."

"What does our minister think?" bluntly asked Mr. Sampson, "we do not want to propose any
revival measures to our people which he does 'nt
approve of."

" The value of protracted meetings," said **Mr.**
Holbrook, " in my view, depends very much upon
the evidence of success attending the *ordinary*
means of promoting the interests of religion.   I
have given the subject a good deal of thought with
reference to the wants of our own church, and my
opinion is, that in the present state of things, such
meetings would not be expedient."

Deacon Silas moved uneasily in his chair.   Mr.
Lovering put one foot over the other, then changed
it back again.   Mr. Sampson looked up disappointed, but inquiringly at Mr. Holbrook.

" I am sorry you think so," said Mr. Lovering,
who had very much at heart the selling of the
pews of the Downs Street Church, and felt that in
order to accomplish this, a *stir* must be made
about something.   " I do n't know of anything
which does more for a church than a *good rousing
revival.*   It fills a meeting-house up, Mr. Holbrook,
and a church that *is* anything in these days, is expected to have revivals.   People must see something going on in the religious line, or they won't
have anything to do with religion.   It would tell
well for us to have a series of meetings, and send
notices around to all the papers ; and get famous
preachers here ; and have the music spruced up
a little ; it would draw attention to us, and that is
what we want.   We are out of the way, and if

folks won't notice us, we must make them, — so the world goes."

" Brother Lovering," remarked deacon Silas, " I do not know that we need put ourselves particularly out of the way to attract notice. If we can agree on any such measures as will satisfy ourselves, I shall be content."

" Well, deacon," said Mr. Sampson again, bluntly, " what would you like ?   Our minister does not seem to fall into our plan of protracted meetings, and I, for one, depend upon his judgment in the matter. I suspect he knows more about such things than we do, — now what will you have?"

Deacon Silas cleared his throat, for in damp weather he was troubled with the asthma. What " he would have," it was difficult for him to say. His notions of the sovereignty of God, in the production of revivals, were confused. He seemed to regard them as something like a political excitement, or a fever of speculation, — dependent on certain *expedients*, which, if vigorously used, would certainly, " get up a revival." He sometimes gave evidence also, that he was not yet prepared to be " translated;" for his wishes, like many others which come from a partially sanctified heart, were mixed, — nature and grace struggling together for the victory. He wished to see people converted, but it pleased him best when conversions were

15*

made under measures in which he took the lead. He thought he had the "gift of tongues," and he was never more in his element than when he exercised it for the edification of his brethren and others in times of religious excitement. That the cause of religion should prosper, and yet in a way which should make a great man of him, was his most sincere desire. The little human heart is wonderfully deceitful, and whether the one the deacon laid claim to ever let him into its secrets, is not known. If it did, he took care not to reveal them. To the question, "What will you have?" therefore, there was no reply, but the clearing of the asthmatic throat.

No one else seeming ready to speak, Mr. Sampson continued : "As you say, deacon Silas, we must agree among ourselves, and now what I want is, to wake our people up so they will listen to the preaching. I do not care how it is done, whether by protracted meetings, or inquiry-meetings, or morning prayer-meetings, but on some measures," —

"That's it," broke in Mr. Lovering, "*some* measures which will put us all to work, and make a talk. There is a great deal in making a *talk*, especially in a city. Why, if you put a notice in the paper that a preacher has a remarkable nose, everybody will run the next Sunday to see it, and then he has a fine chance, you know, to give them good Bible-doctrine, and ten to one, they will go away better than they came. Now, Mr. Holbrook, as you do n't like protracted meetings," —

"I did not say I did not like protracted meetings, Mr. Lovering, you are rather too fast for me; I simply said that in the present condition of our church, taken as a whole, I think such a measure inexpedient."

"Well," said Mr. Sampson, "we all feel, or ought to, that you know better what we need than we do ourselves."

Deacon Silas again cleared his throat, though by no means as a sign of assent to brother Sampson's remark, and then said, "How would the plan strike you, sir, to hold a series of daily prayer-meetings ?"

"If any considerable number of my people," said Mr. Holbrook, "wish to come together for daily prayer, or if any wish to meet their pastor for the purpose of religious conversation, I am not only willing, but shall be glad to aid them by every means in my power."

"That's it," said Mr. Sampson, "that's all we want; we have the same object at heart all of us, I suppose, to help a fellow-traveller on to heaven, and for my part, I feel safer to follow where my minister leads. Let us have the prayer-meetings, and follow them up close with inquiry-meetings, and if we are faithful in our closets as well as in the vestry, I've no doubt God will bless our efforts."

" We had better put notices in the papers, I think," said Mr. Lovering, " that we are to hold a series of extra meetings, and when they are to commence, and if Mr. Holbrook can, it would be a good plan just to state the subject of the next Sunday's sermons, and have them something rather taking to begin with, — something out of the common way."

To this deacon Silas objected, and spared the minister the trouble. Mr. Lovering looked disappointed, but did not press his point, and soon interested himself in the detail of the arrangements of the proposed meetings for prayer and religious conference. This was accomplished to the satisfaction of Mr. Sampson, and the acquiescence of the other gentlemen; Mr. Lovering, however, persisting to the last in the opinion, " that it was a great mistake not to get 'em into the newspapers."

Mr. Holbrook began to converse on other matters; but every subject which he introduced fell flat. The object of the interview was, evidently, not all disclosed, — the deacon had something more on his mind.

Distantly and guardedly he approached his object; his caution was too much for Mr. Lovering's patience, and after bearing it as long as he thought courtesy demanded, he broke the ice at one plunge.

"Mr. Holbrook," said he, "I would n't on any account seem to be finding fault with my minister, but do n't you think a little different sort of preaching for awhile, just in our present emergency, would be a good thing?"

"What kind of preaching would you have, Mr. Lovering?"

"Well — what we have now is most excellent; I always enjoy it, and it does me good. But people are not all alike you know. Now do n't you think if you would, for a spell, talk up to folks a little closer, and make them feel they are sinners, and must attend to't right off, do n't you think we should have more awakenings?"

"I suppose," said deacon Silas, caressing his knee affectionately, "that *you* think, brother Lovering, it would be profitable to suspend doctrinal preaching for awhile, and have a course of hortatory sermons?"

"Exactly! that's just what I meant to say," replied Mr. Lovering to the deacon's remark, which though apparently aimed at him, was intended for the distant corner where the minister sat.

"I do not know but such a course of preaching would be judicious," said Mr. Sampson, "there are some minds which you cannot get at, except through the heart; you must make them feel, before you can make them think ; but on this point, brethren, I for one, do not feel capable of advising my minister. I would rather trust his judgment than my own. The conversion of our people is as dear to him as to us."

"Yes," said Mr. Holbrook, in a pleasant tone, "we all have the same object in view, but we differ a little, I see, in our judgment as to the best means of accomplishing it."

"There is no help like *experience* in forming our judgments," said deacon Silas, emphatically.

Mr. Holbrook bowed, and went on with the conversation as if he in no way appreciated the thrust at his youth.

"I believe," continued he, "that the best way of making men feel *intelligently*, or with any great depth of sensibility, is to make them *think;* and to make them think *and* feel, you must give them preaching which is at once instructive and earnest."

"But, Mr. Holbrook," said Mr. Lovering, "need we preach about the *doctrines* all the time to do that?"

This remark pleased deacon Silas. It was quite

to his mind, when he could keep behind the curtain and pull the wires. Such a man as Mr. Lovering would go off, if somebody primed him.

"No, not *all* the time," said Mr. Holbrook, smiling, but suddenly the grave expression of his countenance returned. "I do believe a thorough and correct discussion of the great doctrines of religion to be the great staple of the pulpit everywhere. They are so in all the preaching recorded in the Bible."

"For my part," said Mr. Sampson "this is the kind of preaching I like to sit under; but is it so with the common run of hearers?"

"Indeed it is n't," said Mr. Lovering; "I can testify to that. Most folks go to church because they do n't know what else to do, and if they do n't hear something to keep them awake, they will not try it again in that place — that's all.

"Instructive preaching requires an instructed audience," remarked deacon Silas.

"Do you not think a mistake is sometimes made on that point?" continued the minister. "I have, I must confess, a great respect for the ability of *common minds*. They can and do appreciate such preaching, and feel its power. With an honest conscience, and strong common sense, they do not need clap-trap to impress them. There is many a hard working man in our con gregation, who thinks out his own views in theology. Such men need, and have a right to demand, that strong thoughts shall be given them in sermons."

"But, Mr. Holbrook, what you call 'clap-trap,' I suppose it must be conceded, does impress them. It's the noisy preachers who are most run after."

"Very true," said Mr. Holbrook, and "I am very sorry we must confess it. In our large cities, we are in danger of being overrun by a perverted taste about preaching and preachers. The excitement of a large population, — the bustle of business, — the increase of wealth and luxurious modes of living, tend to create mental debility. This gives rise to a demand for a noisy and declamatory delivery, and for a pretty, affected, mincing style. And to suit these, we must have the glaring and superficial, or the weak and maudlin in sentiment. This will never convert men, nor will it *long* retain them within reach of our influence."

"I see plainly enough," said Mr. Sampson, addressing the deacon, "that our minister will do nothing to help along such a perverted taste. There must be a more manly administration of the pulpit to suit him, and I am thinking he is about right."

"I hope we shall all set our faces against it," said Mr. Holbrook, earnestly. "If the gospel will not affect men, we have little to hope for, from any appendages we can give it."

"These are new notions," said Mr. Lovering, "I am afraid they will not fill up our church."

"As to our church," said Mr. Holbrook, "I think that any attempt to *crowd* it into notice will be impolitic. Such an attempt will create a *kind* of interest among us and around us, which we do not want; and will tend to throw off from us the more intelligent and conscientious part of the community. We shall grow, if we do our duty, and have patience. We must bide our time."

"Well," said Mr. Lovering, coloring slightly, "I hope you have a right notion of it, but when we come to the dollars and cents, that's what *tests* principles best, according to my notion."

"I suppose," remarked deacon Silas, "you will be willing to consult with your people as to the best course to be pursued."

"I certainly respect the feelings and wishes of my people," replied Mr. Holbrook, "and, within *certain limits*, should prefer to consult them; but you can easily see, deacon Silas, that there is a point beyond which the minister is properly his own judge of duty; and, in order to try his own plan of operations, he should be allowed a fair field."

"Just so," said Mr. Sampson, "I agree with
16

you, Mr. Holbrook; "if a people have a minister in whom they can confide, it's their place to give way and aid him."

"And suppose they differ from him as to the expediency of his plans?" asked deacon Silas.

"Then," said Mr. Holbrook, pleasantly, "if he cannot convert them to his views, it is his place to give way to them, restore to them their pulpit, and seek another field of labor."

Deacon Silas bit his lip. His minister was not quite as malleable as he had supposed.

"Well," said Mr. Lovering, rising, "we've about spent the evening I reckon. And the prayer-meetings, when are they to come on? It's a great pity something or other can't go into the newspapers."

"You have a great reverence for newspapers I see, Mr. Lovering," said Mr. Holbrook. "I think editors ought to treat you well." Upon this, his three friends turned to leave him.

"I will see you again, sir," remarked the deacon.

Mr. Sampson lingered a moment in the hall, after the others had left. He grasped Mr. Holbrook by the hand, and said in a low tone, "Keep your own ground, sir, your church are with you, and so am I; only sometimes he, (and he pointed to the retreating figure of the deacon,) he likes to crack the whip a little," and Mr. Sampson went away laughing.

The minister felt little like laughing. The interview had been to him a painful one, — it was the first ebbing of the tide of general favor with which he had been received. As he lay awake, tossing and restless, his excited mind magnified the evil. He began to fear that there was some secret dissatisfaction with his preaching, which had escaped his observation.

The next morning, Lucy observed his depression, and insisted upon knowing its cause. "He had not slept." "Surely, then, he ought not to go into his study, but take the day for recreation and rest." This could not be done, he must prepare for the Sabbath.

"What kept you awake?" inquired she.

Mr. Holbrook would gladly have evaded the question; it was part of his domestic policy not to talk of disagreeable things, when there was nothing to be gained by it; but Lucy would be answered.

"Were deacon Silas and Mr. Lovering satisfied with the result of their call," she inquired.

"The deacon was not, and Mr. Lovering would have been better pleased, if he had made me promise I would put a notice into the papers, that on "Sabbath evening next, a lecture might be expected in the Downs Street Church, on Belshazzar and the Great Dragon, — with original and appropriate music."

" Dear me ! " said Lucy, " I would not try to please him.   Do tell me, if there is not something I can do to help you to-day ? "

" Yes, if you can call and see how Mr. Roberts is, it will save me time; he has been quite ill."

Lucy soon went out, and called.   Mr. Roberts was better, and had gone out to ride, — Mrs. Roberts was in.   Lucy found her sitting, gaily dressed, in the parlor.   She lived in more elegant style than most of the Downs Street people.   She was fond of show, though she was at heart a good woman.

As usual, she began to converse with Mrs. Holbrook on the state of the church.   Lucy immediately felt uneasy.   It seemed to her, as if Mrs. Roberts always had something unpleasant to say about the church.

" We are in a very cold state," she remarked, " I wonder why it is ? I am sure it's not our minister's fault."

" Our meetings are well attended," replied Lucy, " and our people listen attentively."

" Yes, many come," said Mrs. Roberts, " but more stay away.   There is very little interest among us."

" I was not aware of that," said Lucy.

" Yes, it is so.   The truth is, something ought to be done to get up a revival.   Our young folks do need it."

"But the Sabbath school is crowded," persisted Lucy. "Mr. Holbrook visited it last Sabbath."

"Yes, but then Sabbath evenings, there are so many of them walking the streets, not knowing what to do with themselves. If we could only have preaching, and have our church lighted up, it would be a grand thing."

"Mr. Holbrook could not preach a third service," said Lucy, "he is working now to the very extent of his strength."

"We would 'nt hurt our minister for anything; Mr. Holbrook need 'nt preach, if he would only *talk* to them it would be blessed, I do think. Our church looks beautifully when it is lighted up; they have introduced gas lately, you know, — and a bright house catches the strollers."

"Only *talk*," thought Lucy, as she walked home; "it seems to me people have an idea that all a minister need do in order to *talk*, is just to open his mouth; and yet they expect him to talk sermons. Preach Sabbath evening, and have our great church lighted up! I wonder how long he would live, if he tried to suit all of them. Only a talk! Well, — sure enough, it was only the straw which broke the camel's back. I wonder if Mrs. Roberts ever heard of it, or if she ever hears of anything in our church which is en-

16*

couraging.   I will not call there very soon again;
she always contrives to make me feel blue."

Mr. Holbrook noticed her dejected look, and
insisted upon knowing its cause.   Mrs. Roberts's
remarks and the gentlemen's call, put together,
appeared to him to indicate something seriously
wrong.   He began to fear that he was not giving
satisfaction, and expressed his fears to Lucy.   For
once she yielded to them, and they took her cap-
tive.   She went to her nursery and sat down there,
feeling sad.   The Downs Street people, then, were
already complaining!   Mr. Holbrook should not
stay with them; he was doing them no good, and
was working himself to death for nothing.   She
would persuade him to ask a dismission at once,
before things grew worse.   What a disappointment to her.   She thought they were daily becoming more and more united as a church.   A sad
mistake, truly, had she made.   Then they must
leave their people, — Mrs. Kennedy and Mrs. Bent
and Mrs. Vinton and Herbert and dear little
" Number Five," where her baby first saw the
light, and they must wander off seeking a home!
Lucy burst into tears.   There was sorrow that day
at the pastor's, on account of vague complaints,
many of which were thoughtlessly uttered, and
soon forgotten.

While Lucy was still weeping, Bridget came

to tell her that she was wanted in the parlor. O dear! how could she go down with such red eyes! Yet go she must. Her hat and cloak were lying in the chair, and she hastily put them on, that her veil might partially conceal her face. Thus she went down, and found a woman, neatly but cheaply dressed, who had called to see her. Lucy did not immediately recognize her, but soon saw that it was Mrs. Whiddon, a poor widow, whom Mr. Holbrook had befriended when they first came to the city. She had one daughter married, who lived just out of the city, and who frequently, at that time, urged her mother to come and live with her, but without success: the mother's answer invariably was, " I cannot make up my mind to leave the minister." Necessity had, however, at length compelled her to go.

" You do n't know," said she to Lucy, " how I miss my minister. 'T a'nt no Sunday to me, when I do n't hear him. His preaching did me good; it always *larnt* me something, and his prayers used to comfort me all the week. I 've had a good many ministers in my day, for I 've been but a rolling stone; but I 've never had none I think so much on, as I do your husband. I wish our preachers generally would give us more such doctrinal preaching. It does one good. Why, I 've something to think on all the week over my wash-

tub when I hear him.   I can think as well as feel,
and 't a'nt everybody makes us do that you know."

How astonished and grateful was Lucy! Throw
up your veil, desponding one, — the faithful preacher *never* labors in vain.   While the distrustful
tears were yet wet upon your cheek, God sent in
the poor widow to comfort you.   Learn from her,
that His word shall accomplish the thing for which
it was sent, and that those who will sow in hope
shall reap with joy, if they will but remember
that there is a seed-time and a harvest.

Lucy had a long conversation with Mrs. Whiddon.   She found her a strong-minded, warm-hearted Christian, and she felt that they could ill spare
such hearers from the Downs Street Church.   Mrs.
Whiddon, before she left, opened the basket which
she carried, — and handed Lucy a spare-rib, nicely
pinned up in a napkin.   "Her son-in-law," she
said, " had killed a pig, and given this to her; but
she did not set as much store by fresh meat as
some did, and she wanted to bring it to her minister, — it was all she had to bring."   Lucy accepted this gift for him with pleasure.   She also had
a cup of coffee and some cake sent up for Mrs.
Whiddon, and then, as the twilight was deepening, sent her home in an omnibus.

CHAPTER XXI.

DR. BARROWS.

THE minister was told all that the poor widow had said about his preaching. Lucy hoped it would comfort him, and it did afford him a gleam of pleasure, — yet only a gleam, for the clouds were thick about him, and his soul was burdened on account of his people. It seemed to him they demanded a *kind* of effort which he could not make, and that he had been mistaken in supposing they had gained ground under his ministry. At times it appeared to him that there must be a radical defect in the character of his own preaching, and that his modes of presenting truth were not suited to the purpose of impression on the popular mind. His body and intellect having been severely taxed by his new duties, he was unable to meet his troubles with buoyancy of spirit, — troubles which, after all, his people unintentionally gave him. Many, in speaking of the "cold state of the church," attached no definite ideas to their language ; they talked thus from mere habit. Others only gave vent, in this way, to a secret

uneasiness which they felt at their own incon-
stancy of christian character.   Others still, had
an impression that the only way to keep piety
astir, was to have something to contend about, or
some *evil* to remedy.   Yet again, others were
disposed to look unfavorably upon any *existing*
state of things.   They looked constantly for a lost
or an undiscovered treasure.   They felt, that unless something was done which was not done, (it
mattered not much what,) the cause of religion
could never prosper.   Most of these good people
were shooting into the air.   When complainers
have a minister whom they truly value, they must
not " draw a bow at a venture."   A random shot
may wound him when they least intend it, — and
the rankling arrow may make him weary in the
race, — too weary even to ' run with footmen.'
Exhaustion of the energy of feeling on such causes,
will surely abstract something from his mental
energy, and the inevitable result will be seen, in
the dull sermon.

Complaints should be carefully sifted before they
are brought to him for redress.   The injunction
is, " Bear ye *one another's* burdens," not ' cast all
upon one.'   A patient, faithful examination of a
difficulty, will as often send the examiner to his
closet to mourn over his own distance from God,
as to his pastor to complain of the coldness of the

church. Be honest in judging of yourself, and generous in your judgment of others, and you will love complaining less, and secret prayer more.

While Mr. Holbrook was depressed from these causes, his interest in his sermons flagged. One morning, he felt compelled to lay his writing aside, and take up a book. The cheerful shining of the sun seemed to invite him forth, and he sauntered down upon the wharves, where he sometimes resorted for the sake of observing men and things in a new aspect. The change of scene, and a chat which he had with a rough old sailor, and the fresh air, bringing tidings of a coming spring, refreshed him. His thoughts were diverted from their weary round, and he was returning, enlivened anew for duty, when he met Mr. Bolton.

Mr. Bolton joined him, and almost immediately introduced the subject of abolition. On the preceding evening, he had attended an antislavery meeting, where imposing plans of immediate emancipation had been discussed, and fiery resolves passed. Heated to boiling point, when once Mr. Bolton opened his mouth, his feelings boiled over. His emotions almost choked him; words would not form themselves fast enough for his purpose, and he was obliged to resort to violent gesticulations before he could make Mr. Holbrook understand 'that the Downs Street Church were guilty

— wofully — damnably guilty,' in the stand they were taking on this great question; and if they did not come up to their duty, he, for one, should quit, and he knew of a good many others who would do the same.   They would have nothing to do with a church that would "fellowship man-stealers."

"What do you wish *me* to do?" inquired Mr. Holbrook.

"To preach more and pray more for the slave; for him who is ground down into the dust by the iron heel of the oppressor; for him who is chained in the market-place, and whipped like a dog; and sold, body and soul."

"I pray for him every Sabbath," said the minister.

"Yes — in tame Bible language," said Mr. Bolton, with a sneer; "and you pray as much for the man-stealer as for the stolen man.   It's poor stuff such prayers are made of.   God never'll hear them.   He can't, if he is a God of justice. You don't pray as you would if your child was under the hammer; 't would be another story then, I reckon."

Mr. Holbrook's face flushed.   He was not used to being thus assaulted; his first impulse was to turn from the angry man, and leave him; but on a second thought, he answered him calmly.

"Mr. Bolton, let us not forget the courtesy that is due between gentlemen. Come in, and take a dish of tea with me, and I will give you my views of this matter. You will find, I think, that there is less difference of opinion between us than you seem to suppose."

But there was, just now, no reasoning with the hot-headed reformer. His wrath grew the more fiery at the dignified good-nature of his pastor; and they parted, therefore, at the door of "Number Five."

This incident, however, did not add to Mr. Holbrook's depression. True, it made the harness gall, but it galled now in a new place. Fortunately, on the subject of slavery, his opinions had been deliberately formed, and his confidence in them had increased, and he believed that he could commend them to the consciences of all candid men, who cared to know what they were.

He reëntered his study, and returned with roused resolution to his work. His text was chosen, and his plan for a sermon formed; but his mind labored hard at its work, for the clouds still lay heavily about him. His introduction was a weighty one; he strove to mould it into form, but it was obstinate and unwieldy. The minister, in losing his spirits, had lost all mental vivacity; and this subtle essence being absent, his thoughts

17

became like solid and inert matter.   It was in the afternoon that he was thus toiling at his introduction, for two golden mornings of the week had already been lost.   Over the old church tower evening clouds began to blush, and the minister was still toiling.   As he wearily raised his head, his eye fell upon them.   He watched them, deepening and still deepening, — the sun, his day's work being done, was going peacefully to rest.

The view had a magic effect upon the worn man ; it tranquillized his feelings ; it raised his spirits ; it lured his thoughts heavenward.   Why should not *he* also do his work while the day lasted?   The rest and the reward were promised *there*, not here.

Not wishing to write more at that time, he threw aside his introduction, and went out to walk ; unconsciously, he turned towards the setting sun, communing with his own heart, and with God.

In passing a fine dwelling-house, he heard some one calling his name.   He immediately stopped, and was surprised to see the Rev. Dr. Barrows standing near him.   Dr. Barrows had known Charles Holbrook from a little boy, and always met him cordially.   Now, he insisted upon his coming in, and they entered the house together. Mr. Holbrook soon found himself tête à tête with a great man, for Dr. Barrows' praise was in all the churches.   At first, he conversed with diffidence, for his reverence for his learned friend was great; but this gave way before Dr. Barrows' warm and genial manner, and sincere interest in him.

Before long, he was conversing freely with him, and telling him more of his personal trials, in his new position, than he had ever before disclosed to any one but Lucy. He spoke of the difficulty which a young man necessarily finds in taking his true position among his seniors in the ministry; of the expectation of his people that he would lay himself out as a 'popular' preacher, in order to "fill up his house;" of the obstacles which the location of his church presented to its success; and especially, of the discouragement he experienced from the changeable character of the population around him.

"I know all about that," broke in Dr. Barrows; "I begun with just such a church, and have gone on with it to where it stands now. I have been over every inch of the ground, Mr. Holbrook, and I can say to you, never get discouraged. Hold on, — do your work, and do it right, and trust the rest to time and to God. In this constant ebbing and flowing of population, there will now and then be a pearl or a precious stone left on the shore, and you will find yourself in possession of treasures, if you will wait for them to accumulate."

Mr. Holbrook was, of course, very much interested in Dr. Barrows' account of his own personal experience, which he gave him at some length. He had, with sound judgment, and an unprejudiced conscience, first chosen the objects of labor, and then, with remarkable energy and patience, had pursued them; turning from them neither to the right nor to the left. Mr. Holbrook thought, that from this, rather than from any remarkable talents, his success had arisen. The history of it much encouraged him, and it was for this purpose Dr. Barrows spoke so fully of his own experience. He understood the state of mind in which his young friend was; indeed, he well knew how to lead a young man along, without taking him off his feet.

Mr. Holbrook, after this most timely interview with Dr. Barrows, rose to take his leave; but not a word did he say of the Sabbath, which was near at hand. If it was not to be expected that Dr. Dodd should preach in the Downs Street Church, while the pulpits up town were all open to him, it certainly was not appropriate to expect it from Dr. Barrows. The Downs Street minister, therefore, was silent on this point. Perhaps Dr. Barrows understood his thoughts, for he said to him, at parting, " By the way, brother Holbrook, are you ready for the Sabbath? "

"No, sir," said Mr. Holbrook, smiling.

"I shall be glad to preach for you, if you wish it," said Dr. Barrows. Mr. Holbrook joyfully accepted this offer.

"Which part of the day shall I preach?"

"Suit your own convenience in that respect, sir."

"You do not need me all day then?"

"I do *need* it," said Mr. Holbrook.

"You look as if you did, I'll preach for you all day then." They shook hands, and parted.

It was with light and rapid steps Mr. Holbrook returned to "Number Five." Lucy heard him when he entered, and heard him going to his study two stairs at a time, humming as he went. Light was dawning, thanks to good Dr. Barrows, — and thanks to those wooing clouds of evening which lured him from his study, — or rather thanks to Him, whose ministers they were.

The first thing which Mr. Holbrook did, was to take up his profound introduction and read it; the second was, to open his stove door and throw it in. He could write a better now.

17*

CHAPTER XXII.

GRACE WEBSTER.

Mr. Holbrook did not forget his promise with regard to the meetings for prayer and conference, and the result proved that he had better understood the wants of his society than his good deacon. But there were other signs of an increasing interest among them, which he observed with joy. The young men came out in large numbers to hear him preach, and were more constant at his evening meetings, and he frequently observed them taking notes. Occasionally, one or two called to converse with the minister on some point which they were discussing among themselves, or to borrow theological books to be read at home. Sometimes two came together, to bring him a tough question of doctrine which they could not answer, and would frequently quote to him his own words as authority. Such occurrences cheered and encouraged him much, and he regretted that these good signs should be so nearly overlooked by some of his worthy people, particularly by Mr. Ellory, upon whom he called one afternoon.

"Ah!" said Mr. Ellory to him, "what have we done that we should be passed over when other churches are blessed? In some places their inquiry-meetings are crowded, they say. For my part, I think we ought to set apart a day of fasting and prayer. If we do n't do something to bring down a revival, we never shall have one."

Mr. Holbrook expressed his own sense of the need of God's presence with his people, and then spoke of much that seemed to him encouraging in the state of the church.

"Well," said Mr. Ellory, upon whom it did not make much impression, "I am glad to hear of it, but what does it all amount to, if sinners are not converted. We must *do* more. Why cannot we set apart one evening to have a special meeting to pray for a revival?"

The minister expressed his readiness to appoint additional meetings, if the church were prepared to sustain them by their presence, but added an expression of preference for an effort in which he was already engaged to increase the interest of the stated meetings of the church.

With this permission, Mr. Ellory went immediately to work. He called upon many church members, and sought to rouse them to personal

effort; he induced Mrs. Roberts to appeal to the
ladies, and the 'special meetings' commenced with
a very full attendance.

This occupied another of the minister's evenings each week ; but this he did not regret, if he
could speak to willing hearers.

But it soon appeared that the novelty of these
extra efforts detracted from the interest of the
other meetings, and when the novelty ceased, the
crowd no longer gathered, and only a few church
veterans thought it their duty to attend them.
They were, after awhile, suspended, and Mr.
Holbrook became convinced, that more good was
to be hoped for from the steady and faithful per-
formance of their regular duties, than from any
forced efforts on their part, with the design of " getting up a revival." There was a point, beyond
which, to multiply the wheels of the machinery,
was only to obstruct the power that moved them.
He became convinced, also, that many of his people
needed a more *contemplative* christian character, to
fit them for the revivals which they so truly prayed
for. He accordingly aimed at this result, in much
of his preaching at that time. To do so, required
a calm and silent courage which few can understand, but they who have been called to work
against the coldness and suspicion of *good men*.

Mr. Ellory was not well satisfied that his plans

should fail. He wished to throw the blame somewhere. He began to whisper about his fears " that
the Downs Street church had chosen the wrong
man. He was not quite so much up to all the new
measures as he, for one, wished he was." His manner towards his pastor changed, and he became
reserved. Mr. Holbrook met him one afternoon,
and observed this change with pain. Just after
this encounter, he entered Mr. Mayhue's store,
and it seemed to him that Mr. Mayhue, also, met
him coldly. He felt the change in their manner,
and was thinking of it as he walked homeward;
so busily thinking, that he had nearly reached
" Number Five " before he remembered that his
object in going out had been to call upon a poor
sick woman. He returned, and entered the sick-
room. He found no coldness there. The dull
eye of the invalid brightened at his approach, —
a flush overspread her pale cheek, and she held
out both hands to welcome him.

" Dick," said she, in a feeble voice, to her boy,
" set a chair for him close to me, so that I may
look at him all the while he stays; and, Dick, hand
him the big Bible, it is such a comfort to hear
him read out of it."

Mr. Holbrook read a chapter to her. She
then wished him to pray. " Your prayers, sir,"
said she, " do so comfort me. How it is I can't

tell ; but you seem to know just what I want to say, and it's a wonder, too, for you never have been sick and poor and friendless. I can't understand it, unless it is that God helps you."

" Now," continued she, when he rose from prayer, " now you must come again, and come soon, for I live on your visits."

Mr. Holbrook promised that he would do so, and then he walked to the window, to say a word to Dick. A geranium, in blossom, stood upon the window-sill.

" What a fine plant," said the minister, " do you take care of it, Dick ? "

" Now mother is sick, I do; when she is well, she won't let me."

" I set a store by it," said the mother; it was my daughter's; she planted it when a little slip, and now she is away off at the West. There, Dick ! get her letter out of the Bible, and give it to the minister. I know he will like to read it."

Mr. Holbrook stopped, and read the well-thumbed letter through. This reminded him of one which he had already carried two days in his pocket, an important letter it was too. He was growing forgetful; he must go back to the office and leave it.

It was, therefore, late when he again approached his own house. A boy was ringing the bell at

"Number Five." It was Dick, with the beautiful geranium.

"Mother sent this to you," said he, "she wants you to have it. She thought you kind o' took a liking to it. She says you must put it in your study, and per'ps when you look at it, it will comfort you a bit."

"Indeed," said Mr. Holbrook, "I should value it, but I do not like to take it away from your mother; I am sure she will miss it; I think you must carry it back, with my thanks."

"No, indeed," said Dick; "she'd rather you would have it. She will take real comfort in thinking it's in your study; 'cause she said so."

Mr. Holbrook hesitated no longer, but took the geranium from Dick, and carried it to his study. Lucy watered it daily, and thus the widow's little love offering thrived, and many times, — "from sad thoughts brought pleasant thoughts to mind."

Without much to encourage, or much to discourage, Mr. Holbrook was enabled . to go on steadily and faithfully in his labor. Indeed, though he was not less eager to *accomplish* immediate results, he was less dependent upon the excitement of *visible* success; he became more willing to "bide his time."

This was not the case, however, as has been already intimated, with some of the Downs Street

204 A PEEP AT NUMBER FIVE.

people. They were restless, unless they had the very tangible evidence of progress afforded by the rapid sale of their pews, or the occupancy of vacant seats. Mr. Holbrook and Lucy were once speaking of this state of feeling. " It seems to me," said she, " that some of our people,reckon our prosperity as drovers do their cattle, worth so much a head, and know of no other way."

" You must not *say* that, Lucy," said Mr. Holbrook, laughing.

" Not aloud you mean; but it is true. I sometimes wonder that you do not get discouraged; I should. When we are growing fast, it is too bad to have them complain and croak."

" It is only a few who do so, Lucy, and for the most part, they are good men. The error is one of judgment, not of feeling. They do not appreciate those influences of great truths, which are slow and unseen and deep. We are not growing fast, that they would see; but we are growing, silently, in bone and muscle. We are gradually collecting a nucleus of strong, able men, and many of our church members are growing strong in Christian character. That is what our society, with its changing elements, most needs."

A ring at the door cut short this conversation. Lucy looked up, and saw the gloomy countenance of Mrs. John. Her first impulse was to take her baby and run away, for Mrs. John came so often with her doleful stories, she was weary of it. It was the same thing each time. " Her husband was unkind to her ; her son was dissipated ; her daughter, who ruled the house, was ill-natured."

Mr. Holbrook was, at this time, fairly caught in the parlor with her, and he was obliged to sit for an hour, and hear the oft-told tale of unnecessary woe. He endeavored to encourage the feeble faith and love which were still struggling in Mrs. John's feeble heart, and his conversation did her good. " She knew it would," she said, "before she came." Lucy did not remain to listen to it, but slipped out, when she could do so unobserved. In the entry stood a chubby-cheeked boy, whom Bridget had just let in; he had a pan of hot buns in his hand, which he had brought fresh from Mrs. Ellory's oven, to the minister's wife. Mrs. John was so much absorbed in her own troubles, that she did not notice Mrs. Holbrook's absence, and the minister, having said all he had to say, suffered the conversation to languish, — and Mrs. John soon took her leave. More than an hour of his precious time had he spent with her ; but she returned to her comfortless home a more patient woman ; her piety had been fanned into a feeble flame, and for a season it did throw its flickering light, silently and genially, on those around her. Yes, an hour

18

of his precious time 'thrown away;' and yet, when that comfortless wife and mother bore up a little more hopefully under life's load, because of that hour ; and when through stormy and weary days she was enabled to do some little honor to the cause of Christ, because of that hour, — who will venture to decide how it might have been better spent?

It was late when Mr. Holbrook entered the ministers' meeting. They had been arranging plans for the benefit of a portion of the community whom they had thus far failed to reach by the ministrations of their pulpits, — plans in which the coöperation of the churches was to be requested. Mr. Holbrook, not having been present to represent the Downs Street church, no portion of the contemplated labor had been assigned to them. It was not until he had left the meeting, and was walking home alone, that this accidental omission presented itself in such a shape as to trouble him. Some of his uneasy friends might feel themselves slighted by the arrangement, — particularly his late adviser, Mr. Lovering, who was so uncomfortably anxious to push the church into notice. Absorbed in these thoughts, Mr. Holbrook unconsciously passed " Number Five," and soon found himself near old Mr. Webster's. He entered the side yard, and lifted the huge knock-

er; he was soon ushered into a quiet sitting-room.
The old gentleman, who was very deaf, sat by
the window reading his newspaper; on the table
before him were four little piles of nuts, each pile
half covering a fig.   Mr. Webster rose to welcome
his minister, and then pointed to the treat, saying,
laughingly, "The rogues run right to me, the
minute they get home from school.   Grandpapa
must have something for them, — it's about all I
do, afternoons, to get these ready."   Mr. Holbrook,
in reply, inquired after each of the children, and
just then Mrs. Webster entered with the eldest
daughter, a young girl about sixteen years old.

Grace Webster was very engaging in her appearance; her manners were gentle, and she was as
timid as a fawn.   Mr. Holbrook was at once much
interested in her; he tried to converse with her,
but could induce her to say but little.   Her mother,
who had been watching her with intense feeling,
at length spoke of the recent interest manifested
in the church meetings, and of the seriousness of
many of the young people, — "and our Grace,"
added she, with a faltering voice and a burst of
tears, "and our Grace wants to talk with you."
Upon this she rose, and immediately left the room.
Old Mr. Webster seemed to understand what was
going on, for he resumed his seat by the window,
and his newspaper.   He was very deaf, and Grace

was now alone with her minister, who at once understood and entered into all her feelings. He seemed to know just what she wished to say. Step by step he gently led her on to breathe out that confession which, as yet, she had dared only to whisper in her closet to God. Her color came and went, — her breathing was rapid, — her heart beat quickly, — and her deep blue eye dilated with intense feeling when the young hope, just born in her heart, found a voice; when she ventured to speak of it to her minister, and say that she hoped she had been forgiven, that her name was enrolled in the " Lamb's book of life." From that moment new ties bound her to him. Her fears vanished, and, looking up into his face with her earnest, tearful eyes, as a daughter looks to her father, she opened to him all her heart. She told him of ' her joy, now that she had found her Saviour; how much she had pined for just such a friend, and that she now found in Him all and more than all she had been seeking, — perfect fulness of sympathy and love. Was it not kind in Him, to come and thus fill her heart; — she asked, was ever love like His? — how had she lived so long without Him?' "And yet," said she, " I think I should have been without Him now, had it not been for you. I was interested in you, and I believed every word you said. When you preached so much and prayed so much about the Saviour, and about trusting Him, I could not forget it. On Sundays and on week days I thought of it, — I knew that I was not loving Him, and I had no peace until I began to pray to Him, and I did pray until I found Him — no, until He found me."

Mr. Holbrook was deeply moved. Grace seem-ed like a daughter to him; and with much of paternal feeling, he gave her such counsel as a young Christian needs. In the midst of this con-versation, the four younger children came romp-ing in from school, eager for their spoils. Mr. Holbrook rose and took his leave, and Grace slip-ped away to her own room, and locked her door, that she might be alone with her Saviour.

Where were now the troubled thoughts which had disquieted the minister on his way to old Mr. Webster's? All vanished, — what could trouble him whom the Master had so signally honored? Nothing; his soul was filled only with thanksgiv-ing that God had blessed his humble efforts to the winning of that *one* young heart to Christ. It was as if an angel ministered to him. He grew stronger for his great work.

18*

CHAPTER XXIII.

A STORM.

One morning, Mr. Holbrook played with his coffee, and ate but little. Lucy observed his worn expression of countenance.

" You look as if you had not slept," said she.

" I did not sleep much."

" You work too late at night; the next thing, you will break down."

" How can I help it? The work must be done, and, yesterday, I was constantly interrupted, and had no unbroken time to myself till after nine in the evening."

" It is too bad," exclaimed she.

" It is not so every day, Lucy."

" It is so often enough to break up half your nights, — do try and eat something. Can't I have anything cooked which will tempt your appetite?"

" O no, — I shall be hungry by and by. I will go and walk, I think."

He went out, and Lucy performed her daily round of morning tasks, somewhat cast down. 'Mr. Holbrook was wearing himself out;' and to her it

seemed the result of inconsiderateness on the part
of his people. They came with such numerous
calls as to break up his day, and crowd his labor
into the night. She felt a little impatience at this;
she was ready to blame them, perhaps unjustly.
Half ashamed and half distressed at a state of feeling which was not natural to her, she thought she
would escape from it by making a few calls. Equip-
ping herself, she went out, and, without any deliberate intention, was before long entering Mrs.
Talbot's cheerful parlor. She sat down in a luxurious arm-chair, and, as she conversed pleasantly
with her kind friend, she watched the blaze shooting up and spreading out and playing pranks over
the handsome logs which had been given it as its
prey; and she was reminded of her old home, —
of the crackling fire in the old kitchen fireplace,
where she had sat many an hour dozing and
dreaming. Mrs. Talbot, also, seemed almost like
a mother to her, and she was allured to make a
confession of her impatient feelings.

"Sometimes, Mrs. Talbot," said she, "I am
afraid I shall never be good enough for a minister's wife, — I am too young and inexperienced."

"You are fast getting the better of that," said
Mrs. Talbot, smiling, "and to us all is promised
strength for the day, — we are sure of so much."

Lucy was of a hopeful temperament, and she

caught at a sunbeam, whenever it was offered to her, — thus, when her call was over, she found herself in the light again. She looked so cheerfully upon John, who stood ready to open the door for her, that he made up his mind that " she was about the handsomest lady he knew."

Lucy next ran in to see Mrs. Kennedy, for she wished to learn if there were any calls which ought to be made among her people. Mrs. Kennedy told her that Mrs. Bent was ill, and accordingly she went there. Mrs. Bent, after awhile, began, as usual, to talk about her minister.

" Does he keep himself well ?" inquired she.

" Pretty well," said Lucy, " sometimes he gets worn out, as I suppose all ministers do."

" You mustn't let him wear himself out," said Mrs. Bent, " we all love to hear him preach, but he mustn't kill himself to please us; tell him to exchange more. He looked pale last Sunday."

" Why, — did he ?" said Lucy, somewhat startled, " well, he wrote late Saturday night, and that will account for it."

" He must not do it," said Mrs. Bent, " and you tell him so, will you? Ask him to preach over his old sermons oftener, — those which he preached when he first came here. You don't know how we all liked them; we had as lief hear them twice a year as not."

"Oh, he has burnt them up," said Lucy, laughing.   Mrs. Bent looked aghast, — 'she could not have it so.'

"You do n't know," continued she, "how much Mr. Bent and I thought of his last sermon.   I have heard a great many of our people speak of it.   We have a young man boarding with us, who is a great reader ; he came home and said, that sermon had settled his mind on the subject of the atonement."

Mrs. Bent was one whose countenance had usually been dark on 'exchange Sabbaths,' and Lucy was therefore surprised and cheered by this conversation.   Upon going into the street, she saw Mrs. Roberts walking slowly, a little before her.   Not wishing to overtake this lady, lest some croaking might disturb her comfort, she turned down into another street, and made a call on Mrs. Robson.   Mrs. Robson, in speaking of her pastor, had always one style of remark, which she never varied.

"What *beautiful* sermons we had last Sunday," said she to Lucy, "I do think Mr. Holbrook is a beautiful preacher, and a beautiful man, — indeed we all think pretty much so.   He does give us such beautiful prayers too, — do n't you think so ? "

"Well," said Lucy, coloring, (what *did* Mrs.

Robson mean by 'beautiful?') "I am glad you were pleased."

"O, yes ;" Mrs. Robson was perfectly convinced that her minister was the most 'beautiful' of all beautiful things.

It was nearly dusk when Lucy reached home. She had been gathering honey in her roamings, and this she spread before the minister at tea. It took effect, though he was unconscious of it, and would not probably have attached much importance to it ; it did sweeten his toil ; he worked the better the next morning in his study, for the consciousness that he had the confidence of his people. It encouraged him to know that one of his doctrinal sermons, which had cost him so much unappreciated toil, had fixed the opinions of at least one young man on the great subject of 'atonement.' Who could tell what that young man might become ? Does not all destiny hang on such turning points ? Mr. Holbrook was learning more and more patiently to labor for hidden results. And yet, was he not doing it at the expense of many of his great plans of study ? He could not find time for all things, and in making his choice thus far, it had always been in favor of what seemed present and pressing duty. Of the future, when his resources should become exhausted, he did not like to think.

One morning, two gentlemen called on Mr. Holbrook. One of them was a physician, and the other was a lawyer. They wished to make inquiries about the Downs Street Church, for they were about to commence the practice of their professions in the city. The real object of their inquiries was to learn, if they could, whether it would assist them, *professionally*, to join Mr. Holbrook's church. He soon perceived this, and was frank with them. He told them, that his people were neither rich nor fashionable, nor in any way 'influential' in the community; that, in a worldly point of view, it would be of no direct advantage to them to join his church; but if they wished to throw in their religious influence where it was most needed, he believed they would find their place among his people, — for young men of education, with families, were greatly needed among them. Now, both of these gentlemen were professing Christians. The doctor, in thinking the matter over, was influenced by Mr. Holbrook's suggestions; he did wish to do good, and, waving all professional advantages, he threw in his lot with the comparatively poor and struggling church. The lawyer, — or the lawyer's *wife*, — concluded that, all things considered, it was their *duty* to go 'up town.' They thought the 'leadings of Providence,' pointed decidedly that way.

This little event was soon followed by trouble. A storm was brewing for the Downs Street minister. Mr. Bolton had, ever since his casual interview with Mr. Holbrook, preserved his boiling temperature on the subject of slavery. A sermon, preached about this time, furnished an unfortunate provocation to his morbid feelings, and, early on Monday morning, he called, in great agitation, upon his pastor.

Scarcely were the courtesies of meeting exchanged, before the subject of yesterday's sermon was introduced by Mr. Bolton, and he was hardly respectful in expressing his dissent from the opinions it contained.

" What are your objections to the sermon?" inquired Mr. Holbrook; " let us see if I have made myself understood? I cannot but believe we *think* substantially alike, though we may not *feel* alike."

" No, sir, neither, I hope. That sermon was pro-slavery, — entirely pro-slavery, sir; it was a disgrace to a christian pulpit, sir; and I have come, sir, to ask that it may be printed. It's high time the northern pulpit were exposed on this subject, sir, — and " —

" Mr. Bolton," interrupted the minister, laying his hand gently upon the angry man, — "this is useless. You are not calm enough to discuss this subject now. Come at another time, and let us talk it over like christian gentlemen."

"No good can come of that, sir; it's too late. I only want your sentiments given to the public, sir, so that they may be answered, and their fallacy exposed, sir. You ministers talk there, in the pulpit, and nobody answers you; and three quarters of the people, poor fools, take it all down as gospel, sir; thank God, the other quarter have more sense. Let your views be printed, and then see what becomes of them, sir."

"That is impossible, Mr. Bolton; if you wish for nothing but that, you have my answer; but I should be glad to" —

"Impossible? I thought so, sir; you dare not meet honest men in argument on the subject, sir; that's the way you all manage, sir; it's a burning shame, sir. For one, I think, sir, the people who employ you have a *right* to demand that such sentiments be uttered where they *can* be answered, sir."

"I have no sentiments to conceal on this subject," replied Mr. Holbrook; "if you wish, at any time, to know my views, I will give them to you; and" —

"I know them already, sir; it's for others I want them."

"Very well, — I was about to say, that if any

of my people wish to know my views on this or
any other topic of similar character, I hold myself ready, as their religious teacher, to tell them
what I think, and why. Beyond this, your good
sense must teach you, that 'rights' and 'demands'
have little to do with the matter."

"Will you take *that*, sir, as containing *my* views
of the whole posse of you? — good morning, sir."
And thus saying, Mr. Bolton drew from his pocket
a pamphlet bearing as its title: "The Church a
Brotherhood of Thieves," — and laying it upon the
centre-table, abruptly took his leave. "Poor fellow," said Mr. Holbrook to himself, when his visitor had disappeared, "he knows as little of his
own heart as he does of mine."

Now the truth was, that in opinion upon the
leading principles involved in the antislavery con-
troversy, the minister and his parishioner did not
essentially differ. Mr. Holbrook, it happened,
was the unknown author of several articles which
had been published on the subject, and of which
Mr. Bolton had but a short time before spoken in
high praise. The only real points of difference
between them were those of secession from the
fellowship of Southern churches; and of a pastor's
control over his own pulpit in the matter of in-
viting a Southern clergyman to occupy it. On
neither of these points could Mr. Holbrook aban-

don what he deemed the liberal and just principles of the Northern churches.

Mr. Bolton was, from this time, an active dis-
turber of the peace of the Downs Street church.
He neglected his business, and, going about hither
and thither, he succeeded in awakening a violent
and factious spirit. It was curious to observe the
elements as they gathered around him, like clouds
when a storm is brewing. One or two supported
him from personal friendship, — and there were
others who were *born* reformers, — and here were a
brace of idlers who entered into the excitement,
as boys do mischief, for the want of something
better to do, — and there were a few conscientious minds who, before they were aware of what
they were a doing, found themselves committed to
plans which they never would have devised coolly.
Thus the dissatisfied numbered more than was
expected. Yet their number was comparatively
small. The great majority of the people stood
shoulder to shoulder with their minister. The
minority asked and received a dismission from
the church, with the exception of Mr. Bolton,
who withdrew from all connection with churches,
and gave himself up to antislavery as to a mono-
mania.

Among the wanderers were some whom Mr.
Holbrook had always regarded as his special

friends, and many whom he loved, and from whom he parted unwillingly. It was a severe trial to him, and he found himself compelled to do, as ministers often must, — take up his wounded affections, and bury them privately at dead of night.

One morning, Mrs. Ellory, whose husband was among the number of the seceders, came in to see Lucy, and sat and wept like a child. "She did love her minister and her church," she said, " and the trial of leaving seemed greater than she could bear. Her children, also, had become attached to the Sabbath school, and they were taking it much to heart. She wished people would n't talk abolition to her husband, it always got him so excited, — he did n't know what he was about; and then he did things which he was sorry for. For her part, she was as sorry for the slaves as any body, but she could n't see what good it did them to run crazy about them; she'd always seen that Mr. Ellory worked the best when he was quiet. "But there," said she, " some folks think it is doing God service to get into a *stew* about a good thing, and go to scolding other people over it."

Mr. Holbrook came down, and when he entered the parlor, Mrs. Ellory could scarcely speak ; — just at this time Mrs. Bolton came in, and it was a painful interview to all. Lucy was glad when it was over, and they rose to go. Mrs. Holbrook attempted to cheer them, and spoke of a brighter future. Mrs. Bolton shook her head; she had suffered long, — they parted from their minister and his wife with tears. Mrs. Bolton, particularly, looked pale and desponding. She had so often been driven from one church to another by this very cause, that she was now utterly cast down. It seemed to her as if, just as soon as they had become attached to friends in one place, her husband took offence at something, and was off to another. Thus there was unusual sorrow at the bursting of this storm.

19*

CHAPTER XXIV.

OLD MR. WEBSTER.

At the close of the week, in which the secession from the church was brought to an issue, Mr. Holbrook was so far exhausted from excitement and anxiety and compassion for the misguided ones of his flock, that he took a violent cold from a slight cause. His throat was affected, and he was threatened with bronchial disease. Lucy's fears took the alarm, and she endeavored to persuade him not to preach; but he was unwilling to leave his pulpit with a stranger at that time. He, therefore, prepared for the Sabbath, and performed his usual services. In the evening, Lucy observed that he made the last prayer as if speaking pained him; and when they came out, she entreated him to cover his face, and go home without talking. As they were going up the steps of "Number Five," they heard some one behind them walking with a cane. Lucy saw by the light of the street lamp that it was old Mr. Webster, and her heart sank within her. He frequently called on Sabbath evening, for he was so deaf

that he could hear but little at church; and he
greatly enjoyed conversing with his minister.
These calls had many times annoyed Lucy. It
seemed to her so inconsiderate in the old gentleman to call when Mr. Holbrook was worn out by
a hard day's work; but never had she been so
much disturbed as on this evening. Now, it seemed to her, not only inconsiderate, but selfish and
cruel; she could not speak to him, but opening
the parlor door, she stepped in hastily, and stood
by the fire, almost ready to cry with vexation.
In came Mr. Webster, following the worn out man.
Lucy did not look up until she was obliged to do
so, and then it was a cold hand which she extended
to the visitor. Her husband saw, at a glance, how
matters were with her, and felt the necessity
of exerting himself. He, therefore, sat near Mr.
Webster, that he might talk with him more easily.
Mr. Webster soon spoke of the late difficulties.

" I thought you looked pale to-day," said the
old man, " and I knew I should sleep all the
better if I just came in to tell you, that those who
have left us are no loss; we shall get along better
without them. We have entire confidence in you,
and, one and all, we mean to uphold you. It seems
as if our people would not be satisfied without
taking some measures to tell you of this, — and
they mean to do so next week. Why, Mrs. Hol-

brook, they are swarming up around your husband like bees around a queen; and I reckon you will hear something of their buzzing before long. Lucy looked up now with a smile, — old Mr. Webster had found his way to her heart, and her ill-humor vanished. His words were as a cordial also to the minister; but they would have benefited him much more, had Mr. Webster reserved them for the morrow. Do not call on your minister Sabbath evening, — let him have rest after his day's labor, — he has well earned it. No matter if it is the most convenient time for you, — remember it is almost an act of inhumanity to him, particularly after his *third* service.

Old Mr. Webster's dull ear did not detect the hoarseness in Mr. Holbrook's voice, and he felt so comfortable before the bright fire, and enjoyed so well the benevolent feeling of which his heart was full, that he made a long call, and soon entered on his favorite topics of conversation, — " Election and — Perseverance."

" O dear," said Lucy, in an under tone, " he has started on election, — shall we have them both ? "

" Hush ! " said her husband.

" He cannot hear me. Do let him do the talking, and you keep still; you have said all you have to on those things, again and again."

Mr. Holbrook did not mind a word she said.

" There," said she, interrupting him again, " you are very hoarse, you ought not to speak another word ; let me talk."

" On Election ? " said he, softly.

" I should think I might," said Lucy, " by this time, I know it by heart."

" I will not trust you, and you must keep still, or I shall laugh."

" Come," persisted Lucy, " change places ; you can prompt me in a whisper if I do not get it right. Try me." Lucy broke into one of her merry laughs ; — soft, but very merry. It once won the heart of the young student, and it had been music to the young pastor. It had been a gleam of sunshine in his city home — chasing away fear and doubt — and sometimes even pain, — clear and silvery it rang, as if from the heart of a little child ; and Lucy still retained a childlike fresh- ness of spirit and cheerfulness, — which were in- valuable in their effect upon the city pastor. But musical as was that laugh, Mr. Webster's ear was deaf to it, and he did not, therefore, precisely un- derstand the connection between his lengthy remark on perseverance, and the fact of Mr. Holbrook's rising abruptly and going to the china-closet. This break-down, however, gave him time to reflect that the night was passing, and on looking

at his watch, he was surprised to find the hour
hand getting far up towards the midnight, — so he
took his leave.

Before Bridget began to lay the cloth for dinner on Monday· morning, the buzzing of the bees,
as Mr. Webster had predicted, was heard at
" Number Five."

Mr. and Mrs. Kennedy called first to say, that
the Downs Street people wished to make their
minister and his wife a donation visit, and their
first object was to ascertain if such a movement
would be agreeable to them.   This was a sponta-
neous expression of the affection and good-will of
the people, and Mr. and Mrs. Holbrook could not
be otherwise than gratified by it.

In a few hours after this plan was generally
known in the society, there was a great stir.
Again young ladies and children were on the
wing, to and from " Number Five," where great
preparation was made for the occasion.   Bed-
steads were removed, carpets covered, tables set.
Then presents — presents — presents, came pouring in.   On the evening before the great day,
Lucy was told that a lady wished to see her in
the entry.   She went down, and found Mrs. Bolton there.

" My heart is with you," said Mrs. Bolton,
slipping at the same time a little bundle into her

hands. "My heart is with you, though I cannot be. My children would not rest until they had done something for to-morrow, — so I brought their work round for them."

"How are you getting along now?" kindly inquired Mrs. Holbrook.

Mrs. Bolton shook her head mournfully, — the bell again rung, and wrapping her cloak about her, she stepped out as some one else entered. Lucy opened the bundle under the hall lamp. It contained half a dozen cravats, nicely hemmed and marked, and some very beautiful lamp-mats. Neither gold nor silver could have affected Mr. Holbrook as did this expression of an attachment, which had survived a rough storm.

The next day was a delightful one, and the donation visit passed off remarkably well. All seemed to enter into it heartily. In the evening, after the crowd had dispersed, Mr. Holbrook and Lucy went up stairs to look at the table, where the gifts had been deposited. The Downs Street people, always generous, seemed on this occasion to have outdone themselves; indeed, it would be an easier task to tell what they did not, rather than what they did, bring. There were groceries in such abundance, that Lucy laughingly proposed they should open a store; and yet it had been so managed, that there was no excessive surplus

of any one article. There were carpets, simple,
yet handsome, for the little parlors of " Number
Five." Mr. Holbrook unrolled them, quietly expressing his admiration, but Lucy capered over
them in high glee ; and the baby joined her, laughing with all its little might. After this, Lucy took
up sundry envelopes, and announced, with a shout,
the contents of each ; bank bills, large and small,
were there found enclosed. " There," said Lucy, as
she held up the contents of the last one, " a twenty
dollar bill ; — now, Charles, we are out of
debt, — and once out, we 'll never get in again ;
we know more about living than we used to."

This was, to Mr. Holbrook, a matter of rejoicing ; for debts press heavily on a minister's spirits,
as well as his purse. He knows he lays up
nothing with which to pay them.

The day after this donation visit, found Lucy at
Mrs. Talbot's. She could not rest until she had
gone to tell her about it. Mrs. Talbot smiled
quietly at the enthusiasm of the minister's wife,
who asked, — " Did you ever know so generous
and warm-hearted a people as ours ? — was there
ever another like them ? "

Knowing that it would give Lucy pleasure, Mrs.
Talbot called John and his carriage, and went
around to " Number Five" to see the presents ;
and she appreciated and praised them to Lucy's

content. As for John, he was taken up with the baby, who coquetted with him through her silvery curls, — and, finally, backed up to him, begging to be taken ; thus John's heart was won.

Thanks to the donation party, — Mr. Holbrook did pay off his debt, and yet have something left to invest at the bookstore. He re-arranged his library, and, with cheerful zeal, at length commenced some of his favorite plans of study, which he had contemplated at respectful distance for a long time. Many of his causes of anxiety with regard to his people had been removed ; many interruptions and demands upon his time, experience had taught him to arrange and systematize, so that they were less annoying to him, and his time was more at his command than it had once been. Thus far, all seemed favorable for study, and he needed no incentive to it ; he was eager for it, for he asked himself, " How shall I keep pouring out, if I never pour in ? " His thirst for study increased when he began to indulge it, and his minutes became doubly precious.

Thus far, for the most part, he had had little to do out of his own church ; but gradually, as he became known, he was more frequently called upon for extra services. Lucy watched his increasing influence with much interest. She had not, in

20

this respect, been quite as willing to "bide his time," as she wished him to be.

She said to him once, " You puzzle me frequently."

" Why ? " he inquired.

" You exhibit now such a quiet self-reliance, and you used to be so timid; what has changed you ? "

" Necessity, if I am changed," said he ; " after a man is fairly launched into the world, he must make up his mind that he must find his level; all I wish now, is to do my work to the best of my ability. I find there is a good deal of pride, sometimes, at the bottom of a young man's humility."

" Are you sure," said Lucy, laughing, " that you and the student I used to know, who roomed in the ' corner, third story, front,' are one and the same ? "

" He has grown older, at any rate ; but, by the way, Lucy, did I tell you I had been invited to preach Mr. Croly's ordination sermon ? "

" No; shall you do it ? "

" I have not fully decided, but I think I shall."

" Would you preach an old sermon?"

" No; I must write a new one."

" How can you find time ? "

" I must find it, if I undertake the matter."

CHAPTER XXV.

INTERRUPTIONS.

MR. Holbrook, having decided to preach at the ordination, his studies were laid aside, and his time was devoted wholly to the sermon for that occasion. He soon became absorbed in it, for he had but a single week in which to write it. On Wednesday, Lucy being out, Bridget called him down several times to see visitors. "Once," said he, in telling Lucy of it, "once it was only a book agent, and I could not get rid of him."

"Why did you not tell him that you were busy, and did not want his books," said Lucy.

"Because he was a good-hearted man, and he had written a memoir of his son and daughter, and I had to listen to the story of their life and death, and buy the book into the bargain."

"It is too bad," said Lucy, "what right had he to your time? What is the need of book agents in a city? we can buy all we want almost at the next door."

Before Lucy had recovered her equanimity,

Bridget introduced a suspicious looking personage, wearing green glasses, and carrying a huge portmanteau in his hand. It was, as she saw at a glance, another *book agent.* The minister was again urged to buy a " precious new Commentary on the Gospels." Mr. Holbrook did not wish to buy ; the man insisted that he should look at the book, and began to unbuckle his portmanteau. Mr. Holbrook told him, positively, that he should not purchase, and had no time to look. Then he insisted that Mr. Holbrook should give him a recommendation. This Mr. Holbrook refused to do, and added a little advice with regard to his going among the Downs Street people. By this time, he of the green glasses had become quite angry. " Sir," said he, " I came here to sell my books, not to ask advice ;" and the interview terminated abruptly. On Wednesday, he was again interrupted by two ladies, who would not go away without seeing him. They had just undertaken a benevolent enterprise, which they wished the Downs Street minister to recommend. He had no time to look into the merits of the case, and refused to recommend a thing of which he was ignorant. The ladies were excited by this unexpected refusal, — and they talked as if they never would stop talking. He was not likely to remain ignorant long of anything which had happened, or might be expected to happen to the enterprise. On ran the hour hand of the timepiece, and still on ran the women's tongues. Glad enough was the minister, when even they said their last word, and he was able to return to his study. The week grew shorter, — but a fraction remained. Part of Friday was devoted to his evening service. On retiring Friday night, he set his alarm-clock that it might rouse him at a very early hour on the following morning. The door bell, however, roused him before the alarm. Mr. Holbrook raised the window, and inquired what was wanted? Old Mrs. Hemp was dying, and wanted the minister to come as quick as he could.

"Pray, who is old Mrs. Hemp?" inquired Lucy.

"I'll be there directly," said Mr. Holbrook. "Old Mrs. Hemp, do you not remember her? She is that old lady who came here at the house-warming, and told you about the warning her sister had had."

"O, I remember," said Lucy, "I wonder if she has been warned. You ask, will you?"

Mr. Holbrook hastened away. He found Mrs. Hemp in that chamber which she once described to Lucy, — lying on the same bed where her sister lay on that eventful night. Her sight had failed, but not her hearing. She was able to converse, and at once recognized her minister's voice.

"It is you, is it?" said she.

20*

"Yes," said Mr. Holbrook, approaching her.

"Well, — I am e'en a'most gone; my lamp is burnt out. I had my warnin at four o'clock. My sister came, as she said she would, and rapped four times. I woke 'em up, and told 'em to go for you, for it was all over with me."

The old lady talked so vigorously, that Mr. Holbrook thought there could be no danger of immediate death. He sat down by her, and inquired about her religious feelings, and her hopes for the future.

"My comfort now," said she, "is all in religion. I've had it for many a year. I did n't always have it; but my sister, she was always good. When I stood there where you are, and saw her die, so easy and so comfortable in her mind, I says to myself, says I, 'there is something in religion, and I'll get it, — by George! I'll get it if it's to be had;' and I did n't rest, sir, till I did get it; and it's no humbug; it is what we want to live by, and it is what we must have to die by."

Mr. Holbrook returned home about breakfast time.

"Is old Mrs. Hemp dead?" inquired Lucy.

"No," said Mr. Holbrook, "and I should not be surprised if she survived a day or two."

"Did she have her warning?"

"She says she did," said he, smiling, and then laughing heartily.

"What can you be laughing at?" said Lucy, surprised.

"At the manner in which the old lady expresses herself. She has a great deal of character, and her own way of saying and doing things. She cannot speak as others do, even about dying." He then related her account of her religious experience.

"Have you any doubt that she is a Christian?"

"No," said he, "none at all."

"I will step in and see her before night," said Lucy. But before night, old Mrs. Hemp had gone where time is no more.

Thus that long morning, on which Mr. Holbrook had so much depended, vanished; and it was even after his usual hour when he entered the study. Be considerate of these study hours, good people. You, also, have an interest at stake in that ordination sermon. Give your minister his mornings. Do not interrupt him in working hours. Let your troubles lie over; they will not injure by keeping. Smooth out your own little perplexities; you have more *knack* at it than you think you have. Your joys and your kindness, come with a loving heart to bring before him, — but not in his *mornings.* If he is to do his work as a preacher, he must have that time. Be as generous to him in sparing his golden minutes, as you are in other matters, and all will go well.

Famously advanced the sermon that morning, for Lucy herself stood sentinel at the door, and answered all calls. By Saturday noon it was so far advanced, that Mr. Holbrook felt very unwilling to lay it aside, and prepare for the Sabbath. Besides, he was not accustomed to give to his people sermons, if such preachments can be called sermons, which were prepared in the 'fag end of the week.'

"This afternoon," said he to Lucy, "would be worth more to me than a whole day next week."

"What a pity that you cannot exchange with some one. Is there no one whom you can ask? Then you could keep at your writing."

"No, there is no one in the city, with whom I could exchange so soon again."

"Is there any one out of the city?"

"Yes, within five miles there are two or three who have proposed an exchange with me."

"Cannot I go for them?" asked Lucy, much animated.

"If you can take a buggy and drive out," said Mr. Holbrook, smiling.

"No, I cannot drive," said Lucy, "but why cannot I take Herbert with me? he frequently drives out with his mother."

"You can," said Mr. Holbrook, "if you have a mind to undertake it."

" I will," said Lucy, " and while you get — the
very *gentlest* horse, you know, Bridget shall run
over for Herbert."

Mr. Holbrook consented to this arrangement,
for the occasion was to him an urgent one ; he
was to prepare his first ordination sermon. Bridget returned with Herbert, and Mrs. Holbrook
was soon ready to start.

" What if I cannot get any one ? " said she,
laughing merrily at the thought ; she had no idea
of failing.

" Then I must sit up all night and write, that 's
all," said he.

" I 'll preach myself first," said Lucy. Herbert
touched the horse, and away they went, on Saturday afternoon, to search for a minister.

Herbert was a good driver ; and he made his
way skilfully through the crowded thoroughfares,
and before long they drew up before the house
where the first call was to be made. The clergyman was in, and Lucy stated the case to him.
" He was sorry ; he should have been happy to
have made an exchange with brother Holbrook,
but an aged member of his church had just died,
and he was to preach her funeral sermon on the
morrow."

Lucy was much disappointed, but the exchange
could not be urged, and she entered the carriage
with Herbert, and once more drove on.

"This is our last chance," said she, when they again stopped; "I hope the minister is in."

He was in, and Lucy again presented her cause.

"He was sorry, very sorry, indeed, but he had been out of his pulpit on the previous Sabbath, and he felt obliged to be at home to-morrow."

Lucy's expressive countenance betrayed her great disappointment. She stood, lingering, by the door. "I do believe," said she, suddenly trying to laugh, "that I shall have to preach after all; I told Mr. Holbrook I would, if I failed of getting some one."

"That alters the case," said the brother minister, whose heart had already begun to relent; "if it is to help a lady, I think I must go; so tell brother Holbrook he may depend upon me."

Lucy thanked him, and much elated by her almost unlooked for success, she sprang into the buggy. Herbert followed, and, whipping up the poney, they started at a round trot for home.

"I have about made up my mind," said Herbert, after a thoughtful pause, "that I do n't want to be a minister."

"Why so?" asked Mrs. Holbrook.

"The more I see of them, the more I am convinced they have a hard life of it. Why, in some respects, they are worse off than our cattle, — our cattle have Sundays to rest in."

"I did not know you had ever thought much about any profession yet, Herbert."

" I have, lately, Mrs. Holbrook ; for father has made up his mind to let Mr. Holbrook do as he pleases about my education, and he insists on my going to college; so I am to go. Mother seems to have set her heart on having me a minister, — I am sure I do n't know why, — but father, though he do n't say much, yet I think he would be glad to have me go into business with him."

" You are not very robust, Herbert."

" No, — not very; and that's another reason why I do n't believe it will ever do for me to be a minister. It seems to me they work like dogs, some of them."

" Why, Herbert, where did you get such notions ? "

" Looking on, Mrs. Holbrook, and thinking. You know mother has always kept an open house, — a sort of minister's hotel; and I have seen a great deal of them."

" Well, Herbert, did you ever see a class of men whom, all things considered, you thought were happier than ministers? "

"I do n't know as I ever did," said Herbert, " sometimes when they get together they are real jolly. I've heard them laugh till our old parlors rang again, and I've been in to see what the fun was, but I never could make much of it ; it was all Old School or New School — or Free-will — or some such thing, — or a quiet joke which would n't make other folks laugh."

"Then you are sure, Herbert, that, as a class, ministers are cheerful and happy, and seem to enjoy life more than most men, in spite of their hard work?"

"Yes, I rather think it is so," said Herbert.

"What's the reason of it?"

"That's more than I can make out, Mrs. Holbrook."

"I suppose, Herbert, that when we have once consecrated ourselves to God's service, we are the happiest where we can do the most work for him ; and the harder the better, if we have strength for it. Then there must be real comfort to a man in feeling that he is not spending his life for nothing, — that his *labor* is worth living for."

"I can understand that," said Herbert ; "I often feel that I should n't be really satisfied to live for nothing but to make money ; — I mean if I could do anything better ; and yet I want some. Now my father is not a rich man, and all he has he means to leave his girls, and he says his boys must take care of themselves ; and this is another reason why I do n't want to be a minister. I should n't feel very comfortable to know I was n't laying up a cent for old age, — and that if anything happened to me, my wife, if I had one, would have to keep a boarding-house to get her living."

"I know that, Herbert," said Mrs. Holbrook, with a sigh; "ministers cannot lay up for old age; it is more than they can do to make the two ends of one year meet. There is not much in the profession to invite a young man; all it promises is hard service, and a heart at peace with God and man; but if you are called to it, Herbert, I do not believe you will shrink from it on this account."

"I am afraid you think I am better than I am, Mrs. Holbrook," said Herbert, in a tone of much feeling; "somehow, my goodness does n't last long."

"My dear boy, I think I shall yet hear you preach," said she, laying her hand affectionately on his shoulder. He raised his deep blue eyes to hers, and tears shone in them. His heart evidently was touched, and Lucy felt that the Holy Spirit was striving with him. Silently she breathed a prayer, that now, in the freshness of its morning, that heart might be given to God and his service — forever.

After this conversation, they rode some time in silence. Just at dusk, they entered again the crowded thoroughfare of the city   A continuous stream of omnibuses, carts, drays, and cabs rolled by them. Lucy watched, with an anxious expression, every vehicle which they passed; she was a little timid, and wished to make sure they did not come too near. Herbert observed the expression of her countenance. "Don't be troubled, Mrs. Holbrook," said he, "I never scraped a wheel yet."

"I see you are a good driver," said she, trying to smile; yet she was rejoiced when they arrived safely at "Number Five."

Mr. Holbrook stood at the parlor window, where he had been for some time anxiously watching for them. He instantly opened the door, and when Lucy looked up into his pale and eager face, she smiled, and without waiting to be questioned, said, "Yes, I have succeeded."

"I *am* glad," was the emphatic response.

Herbert was very kindly pressed to come in to tea, but he could not be persuaded to do so. "His mother," he said, "would be anxious, and he would rather run home."

Lucy sat down to a well spread table, which Bridget had prepared with great care. In a high chair sat Miss Tot, who had purposely been kept awake to welcome her mama. After all were seated, Bridget waited at the door. She wished to know if Mrs. Holbrook was pleased with the tea. Lucy observed her standing there. "How nicely everything looks, Bridget," said she; "it is refreshing to come home, and find everything in order; it rests me."

Bridget was repaid, and went, singing, back to her tidy kitchen. Mrs. Holbrook begged that there might be no writing on this Saturday evening, and as she had earned a right to have a voice in the matter, her wishes were regarded. The minister did not return to his study, but throwing himself on the sofa, rested body and mind.

He was also refreshed rather than wearied by his exchange on the Sabbath, and felt quite fresh for his work on Monday morning. On this morning he was uninterrupted until about noon, when he was called down to see a "gentleman, in the parlor, on particular business." The gentleman turned out to be another book agent, who had called this time not to sell, but to give. He presented Mr. Holbrook with a handsome book, bound in crimson and gold. "It had been purchased of him," he said, "by one of Mr. Holbrook's people, and he had been requested to deliver it." Mr. Holbrook, without looking at it, took it and thanked him, and was returning to his study.

"If you please, sir," said the man, "will you write your name on this bit of paper, to signify that I delivered the book safely, for that gentleman frequently buys of me."

Mr. Holbrook's pen was in his hand ; he hastily wrote his name, and gladly escaped to his study. Some time after, he learned that this *honest* gentleman, having thus obtained his signature, took it among the Downs Street people, and thus induced many to buy of him. Mr. Holbrook then looked at the book to see what it was. He found it to be a poor history of the martyrs, embellished with horrible wood-cuts, representing every conceivable torment. Tearing off the bright covers for a plaything for the baby, he put the remainder of the book into the stove, and glad would he have been, could he thus have disposed of every copy which he had been the innocent means of putting into the libraries of his people.

The ordination day approached, and Mr. Holbrook became more and more absorbed in sermon writing. He continued to write and re-write, but he could not please himself.

Leaving him thus occupied, Lucy, on Thursday morning, ran out to take a little walk. She had not gone far when she met a young girl, one of their people, with whom she stopped to speak.

" Are you all well at home ? " she inquired.

" Yes, ma'am," said the girl, hesitatingly.   Lucy

observed her more closely, and saw that she looked pale, and trembled.

"Is anything the matter?" she anxiously asked again.

"Yes," said the girl, "Jem is taking on again, and it seems as if he would kill us all." She burst into tears.

"I am very sorry to hear it," said Lucy.

"O, you don't know how dreadful it is. Mother sits all day long and watches at the window for our minister; she thought may be he would hear of our trouble in some way, and come to us. We all wanted to send for him, but father would n't let us."

"I will tell him," said Lucy, "and I know he will come as soon as he can."

"I wish he would, — I wish he would," said the girl, bursting afresh into tears, and hurrying away, as people began to notice her in passing.

Lucy at once returned, and told Mr. Holbrook what a state they were in at the Smiths. "What can be the matter?" she asked.

"Jem drinks, and sometimes it seems as if they could not live in the house with him."

"How dreadful! I thought he had reformed long ago."

"They thought so too, but this reformation did not last."

" Why will not the father let them send for you?"

" I do not know.   He never will come in to see
me when I go there; but his wife says he gets
behind the door where he can hear me pray, and
they pretend not to notice it."

" I do wish you could go this afternoon and see
them."

" I wish so too, but I cannot, I am pressed for
time."

Lucy sighed, and went out.   Mr. Holbrook
resumed his pen, but he could not write.   The
image of that afflicted mother, sitting at her window and watching through many weary hours,
and watching in vain for her minister, came
between him and his sermon paper; it disturbed
him, and finally he threw the paper aside, put on
his hat, and went to call upon them.

He found the family all at home, and soon
learned that the son was then confined in a room
over head, where he was raging and storming in
a fit of delirium tremens.

Mr. Holbrook sat down in the little back parlor,
and the mother and daughters gathered around
him.   He sought to comfort them in their sore
extremity; he brought them near to Him who
pitied their sorrows, and gradually they became
more calm.

" You will read and pray with us, won't you?"

said the mother.   " Sarah, bring the Bible."   The
Bible was placed on the table, and just then, to
the astonishment of all, the old father came out
from behind the door, and entered the room.   He
brought down his cane with a noise at every step
as he walked firmly in, and for the first time took
his seat by the minister.

"I am glad to see you," said he to Mr. Holbrook, " glad to see you, sir.   We are in great
trouble.   Jem will drink, and now he raves like
a madman.   He was warned enough about it; he
knew it would cost him soul and body, but he
would drink, and now the devil has got him, and
— he may *keep* him.   There never was a kinder
father than I was.   I did everything for him a son
could ask; I don't reproach myself for nothing.
No, — I was a kind father to him, but now," said
he, sternly striking his cane on the floor, "*now* I
can truly say, — *I don't care anything about him.*"
In vain did he attempt to steady his voice, — it
trembled, — it broke down, — he paused, — he
could not then go on.   " And what has done it?"
he choked out at length, — "drink, — curse them
who sell it."   A dead silence followed, — it was
then broken by howlings from that chamber over-
head, which seemed to echo : " *Curse them who
sell it.*"

The old man's head sunk upon his cane.   Mr.

Holbrook, as soon as he could command his voice, commenced reading from the Bible. There was "abiding peace" in the words which he read. Then he brought the weeping family before God, and committed them to Him. The old man never once raised his head through the prayer; it seemed as if he would never raise it more, — he was stricken in his old age, — his only son was a drunkard. Now, in his sorrow, he had no God to go to. He had despised God in his days of prosperity, and God would not come to him, unsought, in his day of trouble.

Mr. Holbrook left them thus, and returned to his study; but it was long before he could bring back his thoughts to his unfinished paragraph.

Soon after this, he called again upon the Smiths, and again found them weeping; but this time all was still in the house, — the contest was over, — Jem was dead.

Such was the history of their first-born. Tenderly had his infancy been nursed. In health, his pretty ways had delighted his fond young parents; in his little illnesses, they had suffered more than he. Through many weary nights had they tended him as only parents can. They had stepped softly about his darkened chamber, — watching every pulsation, every breath, every varying flush, — and hanging on the words which fell from the doctor's lips, as if they were words of life and death. They had poured out their money as freely as water, and wasted themselves to keep alive that feeble spark of life, — and all for what? "O! *to lay their first-born, in his brown hair, in a drunkard's grave!*"

Surely, it would have broken the hearts of those *young* parents, had they been called upon to cover their baby, in his innocence and beauty, with the sods; but what would have been *that* sorrow compared with *this*, of laying him in his manhood's prime, and in "*his brown hair in the drunkard's grave.*" Cease, then, O mother, to agonize for the life of that precious little one. Meekly bow thy head before "Him who seeth the end from the beginning," and gather up all thy strength to say, "*Not my will,* but *thine* be done!" Even yet, the destroyer goeth about, "seeking whom he may devour."

CHAPTER XXVI.

MISS HUBBELL AGAIN.

THÉ ordination sermon was at length finished
and delivered. Whether Mr. Holbrook himself
was satisfied with it, is not known, but it is certain
that all who heard it were pleased, and that the
Downs Street people held up their heads, with an
innocent pride in their minister.

Before long, Mr. Holbrook began to experience
some of the disadvantages of an increasing popularity. He was very frequently requested to
preach before the various religious societies in
the city and its neighborhood. To have complied
with half of these requests, would have been a
serious tax upon his time; and feeling that his main
strength should be expended upon his own pulpit,
he declined doing any more of this work than
seemed absolutely necessary. Invitations of this
kind, however, were continued, and broke in sadly
upon his duties.

On one occasion, just at the opening of one of
the brightest hours in all his golden morning, two
ladies made their appearance at " Number Five,"

and insisted upon seeing the minister.   He came,
but reluctantly.   The lady, who rose to meet him,
was a stranger; but the daughter, who sat near
her, raised a pair of flashing eyes at his approach,
whose fire he had encountered before.   It was
Miss Hubbell, the city-belle, and her mother.   Mr.
Holbrook recognized her at once; but it seemed
doubtful whether she knew him.

Mrs. Hubbell invited Mr. Holbrook to preach
at the anniversary of the "Female Penitents' Society," of which she was a leading manager.   She
made her request with much pomposity of manner, as if she wished Mr. Holbrook fully to appreciate the honor given him in this application.
To her surprise, he immediately declined it; "it
would be quite out of his power to undertake it."

Mrs. Hubbell was, evidently, both disappointed
and nettled at this refusal, and changing her tone
somewhat, she condescended to urge the matter.
She presented the claims of the society upon the
benevolent, and she gave its history.   Mr. Holbrook must know what it had done, and what it
could do, — and she threw away the precious
minutes as if they were drops of water.   When
she paused to observe the effect of her eloquence,
she found, to her continued annoyance, that Mr.
Holbrook stood just where he did when she commenced.

In a sudden flush of anger, she let out the secret; "that she had already called upon five or six ministers, and could not induce one of them to perform the service." Then altering her tone again, she condescended to entreat. At this juncture, her daughter came to her aid.

"I hear that your church is very full, Mr. Holbrook," said she, with a bland smile; "have you any desirable seats vacant at present? Mother and I have been thinking of making some changes, if we can find just what we want."

Mrs. Hubbell looked up, and met a meaning glance from the dark-eyed beauty.

"O yes," said she; "we are looking about to see what we can do; and from all I hear, I do not think we shall be better satisfied than at the Downs Street Church."

Mr. Holbrook bowed. "He should be very happy to see them there." But he could scarcely conceal a smile at the very courteous manners of the city-belle. She was not now talking with a "poor Theologue," in a rusty coat and ragged collar; she was conversing with a city pastor, of whom she had a favor to ask. She praised him, his church, his people, — honeyed words flowed easily; at length, with one of her most winning smiles, she skilfully led back the conversation to the starting point. Would he preach for them?

No ; he was not even to be flattered into it. With
ill-concealed displeasure, the mother and daughter
suddenly took their leave. As the outer door
closed, Mr. Holbrook looked at Lucy, who sat by,
and observing her eyes full of fun, he said, " The
bait would n't take, would it ? " She gave vent to
her answer in a merry laugh.

" The ministers *are* a lazy set," said Mrs. Hubbell, angrily, as she turned the corner. " I should
like to know what they think they are paid for, if
it is n't for preaching ? "

" Where will you try now ? " asked the beauty.

" I do not know ; I have a great mind to give
it up, and go home."

Again rang the bell at " Number Five." This
time three ladies entered ; but they found Lucy
alone in the parlor, for Mr. Holbrook had slipped
out.

Mrs. Talbot and her sister, and a Mrs. Merrill,
the wife of a roving, ever failing merchant, entered together. Mr. and Mrs. Merrill had just
returned to the Downs Street Church, after a long
absence.

Lucy was much gratified at seeing Mrs. Talbot,
for it was but seldom that she called, and Lucy
had many things to tell her and to show her. Mrs.
Merrill being a stranger, it was not unnatural that
Lucy should wish her stay, just then, might be

22

short ; but no such idea had Mrs. Merrill.   There
she sat, engrossing more than her share of the
conversation, and quite ready to take offence if
she, now one of the sovereign "people," should
not receive as much attention as Mrs. Talbot.
Lucy, unwilling to injure her feelings, and hoping
every moment that she would go, addressed most
of the conversation to her; and Mrs. Merrill,
elated by this, began and gave a detailed account
of their family history. Mr. Such a one, fair as he
seemed, was no better than other folks ; he owed
her husband, and would n't pay the first dollar.
Mr. So and so cheated them ; in short, Mr. Merrill was a poor innocent man, hunted down by
other men of business, like a hare by the hounds.
Lucy became fidgety, distressed.   There sat Mrs.
Talbot and her sister, hearing it all, — and it was
not much to the credit of Mr. Holbrook's honest,
generous people.

Mrs. Talbot by this time, however, read Lucy's
trouble in her countenance ; and with quiet dig-
nity, took the conversation to herself.

"My dear child," said she to Lucy, "I have
come to make you a farewell visit."

" Farewell ? " asked Lucy.

" Yes ; I start next week for the South ; my
physicians insist upon this, or upon my spending
another year abroad ; I am too old, now, to leave
the country again."

" What *shall* I do without you?" burst from Lucy's heart.

" I'm sure you cannot want for anything," chimed in Mrs. Merrill, " with so many folks about you as you have." Lucy did not try to reply; she was very sorrowful. " I shall not bid you good-by now," said she, as Mrs. Talbot rose to go; " I can come and see you once more." She was warmly urged to do so. Mrs. Merrill sat some time after the ladies left, pouring out her complaints, to which Lucy briefly replied, " yes" and " no." She was glad to see the last of her guest for that day.

When she told Mr. Holbrook that Mrs. Talbot was to leave the city, he readily sympathized in her sorrow. " I wish," said he, " that you would go up to the bookstore, and select a handsome Bible, in large print, and let Tot take it to John." Lucy was pleased to do this; she purchased the Bible, had John's name written in it, and taking the child with her, went to make her parting call upon Mrs. Talbot.

Mrs. Talbot was surprised, and touched by the warm expressions of gratitude and attachment which Lucy seemed unable to repress.

What, indeed, had she done to excite them? But a trifle, so it seemed to her, and yet her kindness had been no trifle to the minister's wife. She

had found in her the friend she needed. She came
to the city just from school; she was young and
inexperienced; and was placed, without preparation, in the trying situation of a city pastor's wife.
She needed some friend on whose judgment and
kindness she could rely, and Mrs. Talbot had, from
first to last, been such a friend. To her, all nice
questions of propriety and expediency had been
referred; and Lucy, at length, leaned upon her,
and never thought of undertaking anything of
importance without her approbation. To part from
her was, to Lucy, like parting from a mother.

Mrs. Talbot attempted to cheer her. "I have a
delightful plan for you, my dear Mrs. Holbrook,"
said she; "you and Mr. Holbrook and the baby, and
Bridget to take care of her, must come and spend
your next vacation, all of it, with me. I shall
depend upon it; and you are to be my guests,
you know, both going and returning."

Notwithstanding all her exertions, Lucy left
her in tears. John was standing in the entry when
she went out, so she placed the Bible in her
child's hands, who tottled away with it to him.
John took up both the Bible and the child, kissing
her soft cheek, and hiding his face for a moment
in her long curls. The truth was, John had a
weakness about his eyes just then, which he did
not wish to have seen. He thought it was going

into exile, to go South; and when it came to bidding those whom he cared for good-by, he could not control himself.

"John, I thank you very much for all your kindness to us," said Lucy.

John tried to reply, but no intelligible sound escaped. Lucy shook hands warmly with him, and they, too, parted.

Mrs. Talbot went South, and her faithful John with her. God bless her, wherever she wanders, and temper the rough winds to the "bruised reed." Long may God spare her; she is one of his faith. ful stewards, — faithful over many things. Many a timid and downcast one has she lifted up and strengthened, with heart and hand and purse, — ready ever, with her counsel and her kindest sympathy. Without doubt, some minister's young wife, in the city of her new habitation, will have occasion to echo, " God bless her, and John too."

22*

CHAPTER XXVII.

THE DINNER PARTY.

Mrs. and Miss Hubbell did not publish an account of their interview with the Downs Street minister, and he continued to receive many similar interruptions. In one week, four such requests were presented to him; and Lucy said, laughingly, " I don't see but you are fairly in the market now."

Invitations also to preach ordination sermons multiplied; and, had he chosen, he might have had his hands more than full of this miscellaneous business. This, however, did not seem to him in the straight line of duty, — which, in his view, lay direct to his own pulpit; and it was there he resolved to lay out his main strength. He became more and more absorbed in his work, and had at length but little time and attention to bestow upon his family. He soon gave up the marketing, and Lucy took it in charge, as she did every other domestic care. Indeed, though perhaps she would not like to have it known, she had ordered his coats for him, — she could not see him appearing shabby, and she could not make him think to order them. Thus, with her husband, children, people, house, and company, Lucy led a most busy life.

The majority of ladies think, if they have a little family and a house to look after, they have their hands full; if to this they must add the social claims of a numerous society, — the necessity of being always ready for company, — the necessity of making one dollar do the work of two, — the anxiety, constantly worn and never laid aside anxiety for a husband, — heavily laden, often over-worked, and always taxed to the extent of his powers, — most ladies thus tried, would, indeed, feel that their burden was more than they could bear.

And are not ministers' wives, then, heavily bur-dened? Let their prematurely care-worn and anxious countenances, and their physician's bills answer. It is but an act of common humanity for the minister's people to be considerate and indulgent towards her.

The Downs Street people were so to Lucy, — in various ways they lightened her cares and la-bors, and were always disposed to excuse any ap-parent neglect on her part, and to waive personal claims upon her time. They seldom found fault with her; and thus, busy as her life was, she

found much in its passing to enjoy. Necessity
had developed in her an energy, — the seeds of
which had been sown among New England hills;
and though still young and inexperienced, and in
some respects immature, yet a large share of good
common sense, and the impulses of a kindly nature aided her. In addition to this she had the
somewhat rare gift of a cheerful and buoyant temperament, which led her to go singing about the
work of to-day, and trouble none for the toils of
the morrow.

These things did much towards smoothing for
her the "crooks in the lot," yet it must not be
supposed she escaped without trials; she had her
own, and some were of a nature which her affectionate heart felt deeply. She was obliged to relinquish many little domestic enjoyments with her
husband, upon which she set a high value. He
was so much engrossed by his profession, he had
but little time for her, and even when with her, his
thoughts frequently were on his work, and he was
silent. Sometimes Lucy shed tears in secret over
this, but he never knew it. Her heart, when thus
relieved, returned to its cheerfulness; and without a complaint she made this last and most trying sacrifice, the nature of which none could feel
but herself, — she gave *him* up. "If he is to do
anything in life," she said to herself, "he must be

about it. He can't give his time to his wife and his business too. In *vacation* we will make up for it."

Thus on, from sun to sun, worked Lucy, — looking back smilingly on *labor done*, rather than fearfully forward to a mountain yet to be levelled, — and this habit of mind lightened her toils much. Still her very busy life wore upon her, and she was often ill. On one occasion, after she had been confined to her room nearly a week, and had scarcely set her eyes on the busy minister, she said to him, as he put his head in at the door on his way down, " Charles, I wish I were one of your people."

" Why ? " asked he, quite astonished.

" Because you would call upon me then, when I was ill."

Mr. Holbrook took the hint, and replied to it by moving in his table, and writing in the nursery in the afternoon. Lucy did not find the scratching of his pen amusing, and she was in a worry when the child made a noise, and was not on the whole sorry to see the table moved back again.

In the midst of a very busy week, Mr. Holbrook and his lady were invited out to dine with a new comer, a Mrs. Pell. She was a widow, possessed of a large property, and having recently bought a house in their vicinity, she had taken a pew at the Downs Street Church.

Mr. Holbrook was convinced that he had no time for dinner parties, but Lucy felt that they ought to go, and, influenced by her persuasion, he went, but with his head full of his sermon. He was remarkable for becoming. absorbed by anything in which he was interested. Lucy, fearing that all the talking might be left to her, gave him a hint on the subject.

When they arrived at Mrs. Pell's, they found a very large party assembled, and among them several gentlemen whom Mr. Holbrook knew, — but of late he had been so little into general society, that he found it difficult to converse even with them. Now and then he fell into an embarrassing silence. Lucy could not aid him, as she was conversing with Mrs. Pell.

Dinner was announced, and the ceremony of being seated at the table, again annoyed Mr. Holbrook. He seemed not to understand precisely what he was expected to do. After a few blunders, the guests were apparently arranged according to Mrs. Pell's wish. Mr. Holbrook was placed opposite her at the head of the table, and was requested to carve. Lucy would gladly have had him excused, for he was but an awkward carver, but that seemed out of the question. He therefore commenced operations upon the great turkey before him. A sudden, intelligent, troub-

led glance from Mrs. Pell, convinced Lucy that
already had some blunder been made. She
watched Mr. Holbrook with an anxiety which
she could not wholly conceal, — on he went with
his work, quietly resigned, and looking so exceedingly serious over it, that sometimes Lucy could
scarcely refrain from laughing. Yet she knew it
was a *sober* matter — that carving. What would
Mrs. Pell think, to have her minister deficient in
the graces of the carving-knife? *Mrs. Pell* too,
— who had come with all her silver and cut glass,
and had joined the Downs Street Church. *She*
surely must be pleased, for had not Mr. Lupin
long ago said, " They *must* get *genteel* people to
join them?" Yes, it was important what Mrs.
Pell should think. Of no avail would it prove,
should the preaching on the Sabbath make her
thoughtful through the week, — she could never
patronize a minister who did not understand
carving a turkey, — not she.

The fact that Mr. Holbrook's first cut was a
false one, annoyed her so much as to prevent her
starting and sustaining an easy flow of conversation, and the dinner, with its variety, elegance,
and ceremony, passed off stiffly. All felt a sen-
sation of relief when they rose from the table.

Not long after, Mr. Holbrook and Lucy took
their leave, for the remainder of the broken af-

ternoon was necessarily devoted to making calls.
After this, Mr. Holbrook was very frequently
urged by Lucy to acknowledge the courtesy of
Mrs. Pell's invitation by a call. He always
replied, " that he intended to go just as soon as he
found time." She waited for him as long as she
thought it proper to wait, and then went without
him. Mrs. Pell was not very well pleased by
this. She liked Mr. Holbrook's preaching, but
she could not " put up," with his apparent neglect
of her ; she felt that she was entitled to more
deference. He was not, after all, quite as *genteel*
a minister as she wanted. It was important for
her, being a widow, that he should be able to pre-
side handsomely at her dinner parties. So before
his " time " was found to make a ceremonious call
upon her, she decided to remove with her china
and plate, to worship at a more fashionable —
altar !

When her pew was offered for sale, Mrs. Kennedy came to inquire the reason for this sudden
change. Lucy knew of no reason, unless it was,
that the Downs Street people were not fashionable enough for her.

" O, if that is all," said Mrs. Kennedy, " we
will make no objection to the move. We do not
care to have any one who feels much above the
rest of us."

Mr. Holbrook was neither surprised nor disturbed when he heard of Mrs. Pell's departure. The next day, after a pouring rain, a poor widow, not a rich one, called at "Number Five." Lucy, stepping into the entry, invited her in.

"No, I thank you," said she, "I am all wet and draggled. I should n't have come out, only I had some washing I must take home. I want to tell you, — ever since Willy was sick, and the minister was so kind to him, he has beset me to buy some cravats for him to give to Mr. Holbrook. The very first money he earned, nothing would do but I must take it to buy the cravats; he had got his mind fixed on it when he had the fever. He was dreadful sick, and nobody came near him but the minister. To please him I bought them, and I hemmed them as well as I could by candle-light; for I do n't get no time to sew in the day, — and now I 've brought them along. You must n't look much at the stitches."

Lucy opened the bundle under the hall lamp.

In it were two cravats, fine and nice, bought with the first hard earnings of the widow's son. Lucy thanked her, and sent kind messages to Willy, accompanied by a mug of jelly, for his appetite was capricious. The widow went away happy.

On the next Sabbath, nothing could have persuaded either Willy or his mother to have remained at home. With their own eyes must they see if the minister wore one of *the* cravats; they could distinguish it, even across the church. After service, Willy hung about the door; he was not going home without shaking hands with his minister, if he could help it, — not he. And he did shake hands, laughing all the time as if the little matter of the cravats was quite understood between them. The widow stood a few steps back enjoying the scene. She was very glad to have Willy like his minister; she "reckoned it would be the saving of him." Why should the minister mourn because Mrs. Pell was not waiting, on the steps of the Downs Street Church, to be handed by her minister into her elegant carriage?

CHAPTER XXVIII.

FORGETFULNESS.

OUR city pastor advanced slowly, but steadily. He labored to *instruct* his people, and hoped, in this way, gradually to gather about him a band of intelligent, active, well-disciplined men, stable in christian character, and strong in the support of religious institutions. Such a band of supporters he deemed indispensable to the prosperity of the Downs Street Church.

He did, indeed, advance towards this object; but, alas! towards the execution of his great plans of study for his own improvement, he seemed to make no progress. The more he became known in the city, the more numerous were the demands made upon him for extra labor. His mind was so constantly occupied with great concerns, that his overburdened memory became treacherous in its charge of little things. His increasing forgetfulness at length became a source of trouble to him, and yet one which he saw no means of remedying.

Sometimes in the conference-room, he would

put his hand into his pocket for his prepared memorandum, and thus learn that it had been left on his study table. When going up the pulpit stairs, he, once or twice, recollected that his sermon had been forgotten. Lucy gave him letters to drop into the post-office, and found them, weeks after, snugly stowed away in his pocket. She at length made a business of searching these hiding-places every night, and was frequently rewarded for her trouble.

Mr. Holbrook's immediate friends soon learned to excuse this forgetfulness; Lucy bore it with the utmost patience and good-humor; but sometimes cases occurred in which mischief was done. On one occasion, after a very busy week, when Mr. Holbrook went, as was his usual custom, to the Sewing Society, his thoughts remained in his study. He was obliged to make an effort to enable him to throw himself in among his people with his accustomed sociality.

Very many were present on this evening, and among them, Grace Webster.

In the autumn preceding, Grace had been much out of health, and the physicians had advised a change of climate. She went away, therefore, and had been absent about three months. At the end of this time, she had gained so much, her mother consented to her return.

She had come out for the first time in the evening, to this society meeting; for she knew her minister would be there, and she was so anxious to see him she could not be persuaded to remain at home. She stood in one corner of the room, eagerly watching the door, and was the first one who saw him enter. A smile lighted her pale face, and she exclaimed to a friend near her, — " O, *there* he is!"

" Why, how glad you are to see him," said her friend. " Well, — I have not seen him in *three months,*" said she.

Eagerly she awaited his approach. There were so many to speak to him, it seemed as if he never would make his way to her corner; yet he did at length draw near. Now, then, it was her turn. With beaming eyes and glowing cheeks, and a heart too full for words, she held out her hand to him.

He shook hands with her kindly, as he always did. " Grace," said he, " I am glad to see that you are able to be out in the evening. Is your mother here? and how is your grandfather?" Grace turned away with quivering lip. It was well for her that some one else addressed him, for she could not have spoken then. And was *this all!* She had been absent three long months, — and he had no more to say to her! Yes, —

three months, — long to Grace, but like a dream to her busy minister. During that period many of his people had come and gone, and come again; he had forgotten that Grace was among the number. It seemed to him but yesterday that they met, and he passed on with the crowd.

Poor Grace could not bear it. Her eye drooped, her cheek paled again, her vivacity fled; she soon begged of her mother to leave. When at home, she sat down at her mother's feet, and putting her head into her lap, wept like a child.

"Mother, I have been gone three months, and he did not even ask me how I did."

"Why, Grace," said her mother, "he has so much to do, I dare say he did not know you had been away."

"O yes, he did," said Grace, "for I went and bade him good-by." She could not be comforted, — her heart was broken.

"What's all this about?" said the old grandfather. Grace's mother told him.

"Pooh!" said he, "wipe up your tears, child. I tell you he forgot it, I know he did. Ministers can't think of everything. Wipe up, now, I tell you he forgot it, and I will go and ask him if he did n't."

"That he could *forget* her, was no comfort to Grace; but the old grandfather, true to his word, started off early in the morning for "Number Five."

Mr. Holbrook came down to see him, and the old man told his story at once. "Our Grace is a crying her eyes out," said he, "because she thinks you have something against her." Astonished and grieved, Mr. Holbrook inquired what he meant? Mr. Webster told him of the occurrence the evening before at the Sewing Society.

"I did know," said he, "that she went away for her health, for she came to see me; but it entirely slipped from my mind last night, I had been very busy indeed through the day. Tell Grace she must forgive me, or I shall never forgive myself; we must be friends again. She is dear to me. What do you think of her health; is it improved?"

"Her mother thinks it is," said the old man, rising. And then, after a pause, "I've seen more than threescore years and ten, but I think our little Grace will get to heaven before me."

He thought rightly. Grace did not live very long after this. She and her minister became, at once, warm friends again, and she sometimes wondered how she could have been hurt, just because he could not think of everything and everybody at the same time. But he never forgot her again; and he reckoned it among his precious privileges, that he was allowed to cheer that young pilgrim as she went down into the "dark valley," and to witness her triumph there; and to know when, at last, she entered the cold river, and was borne away, that her Saviour, faithful and true, was with her.

Among the shining ones in heaven, a young harper was heard, tuning her harp to the praise "of Him who had redeemed her by his blood,"— and had she not often said, "If it had not been for your prayers and your preaching, I should not have sought my Saviour?"

After Grace's death, Mr. Holbrook seemed to become more interested than ever in his young people. He prayed much for them; he preached to them; he was eager for their conversion. Many were awakened, and among these Herbert and his sister, — and they, at a suitable time, were admitted to communion at that table where Grace had found so much peace. Her death seemed to have opened the gates of life for the companions of whom she had taken leave.

CHAPTER XXIX.

A JOURNEY.

AFTER the excitement and labor consequent upon this revival among his young people, Mr. Holbrook began to be sensible that he was yet in the body. His nervous system rebelled against its task-master, and, in consequence, he became wakeful and depressed. He required rest and change. The weakness in his throat, also, began again to trouble him.

"You will surely get the bronchitis," said Lucy, "if you labor when you are so much run down. Why cannot you go and take a journey?"

"I do not feel as if I could afford it. I need my money more for other things."

"You shall have all my wedding fees."

"That is not worth while; I am not ill enough to need them. I shall be better by and by."

Lucy was troubled. "If you had the money," said she, "would you go and make Mrs. Talbot a visit?"

"Yes, if I had the money, if it were only to satisfy you about it."

"He shall have it," thought Lucy, "I will manage it in some way."

Before she could satisfactorily arrange a variety of economical contrivances which the urgency of the case suggested, Mr. Webster made an unexpected call.

"I've come early," said he, "but I an't a going to stop. I've been to pay my tax-bill, and it was twenty dollars less than I expected; and I did not know what better I could do with it, than give it to my minister." He tucked it into Mr. Holbrook's hand, and began to button up his over-coat.

"O, Mr. Webster," said Lucy, "you don't know how much good it will do us. I was just wanting money."

"Yes, I do know," said the old man, shaking his head emphatically, "my father was a minister, and I know all about it. I was having a talk with Mr. Ellory on my way here, and I said to him, said I, 'our minister's salary isn't what it ought to be; all he can do is to live on it.' Says Mr. Ellory, 'that's all he wants.' Says I, 'no it isn't;'" and the old man brought down his cane with a thump, — "'no *it is n't;* he ought to lay up something for a wet day as the rest of us do. What's to become of him and his family by and by?' 'O,' says Mr. Ellory, 'he must take no thought for the morrow. If he does God's work, God will take care of him and his family.' 'No He won't, Mr. Ellory,' said I, 'if it is our business to take care of them. God won't do any work we shirk off onto Him, if it *is* for a minister, — that an't His way.'" Mr. Webster stood and laughed, and Lucy, with a sudden gush of feeling, threw her arms about his neck.

"If our people were all like you," said she, caressing him as if he were her grandfather, "we never should want for anything."

Mr. Holbrook touched her, — he wished to suggest caution in speaking of their kind and well-meaning people.

"There, Mrs. Holbrook," said the old gentleman, wiping his eyes, which had overflowed; "do n't you see the minister is jealous?" and, with this remark, he slipped out.

"What do you say now, about a journey?" said Lucy, triumphantly.

"I say I will go," said Mr. Holbrook; but his countenance did not reflect the pleasure which beamed in hers. "What is the matter?" she asked.

"Sometimes I am sad, Lucy, in thinking of the future. I am not the most robust man in the world; what would become of you and the children, if I were to die?"

"Dear me," said Lucy, — for to her the future always looked smilingly, — "I never trouble about to-morrow. If worst should come to worst, I should get along."

"Supposing that you were left a widow with six boys, and not a cent in the world!"

"I 'll tell you," said Lucy, with a glowing face, from which the spirit of the old Bay State spoke, — "I 'd send them all through college, and make men of them."

"What would you do it with?"

"I 'd keep boarders, or I 'd take in fine sewing; I 'd turn and twist, and contrive and work, — but I would and should make it out. You need n't trouble yourself at all about your six boys," said she, laughing merrily. "I 'll take care of them, if anything happens to you. Come, it is time to go and pack."

Mr. Holbrook looked at her slight retreating figure. He thought of her toiling early and late, and growing prematurely old, as she tried to get a living out of "keeping boarders," or of her stitching the light out of those soft, loving, hazel eyes, for a mere pittance with which to buy bread for herself and her children. Could he die easy, and leave her pennyless? a hard question, — but could he make provision for her? — this was still harder.

He went to his study, designing to arrange his business for leaving, but Mr. Webster's conversation had left him little heart for it. He was ill; he felt that he was a tenant of a frail tabernacle; he was about leaving home; he should be exposed to perils by land and by sea; it might be that he should never return, — and that unprovided-for future pressed him like a heavy weight. Even should he return, he saw no escape from it; he should work until he died, with only enough for to-day. It seemed to him, that the churches were bound to make better provision for their ministers, — and he hoped, that before his generation passed away, they would awake to an enlightened sense of their duty in this respect. His pen lay on a blank sheet of paper, and he took it up. The thought struck him that he would make a will. He began thus: "To my dear wife, I give and bequeathe my library," — here he stopped; it was all he had to bequeathe; but the will was too short, and he added, — "I bequeathe to her and my children the following: *'I have been young, but now am old; yet never have I seen the righteous forsaken, or his seed begging bread.'*" He had need of faith, more than as a grain of mustard seed, — faith like a huge towering tree, in whose branches the lark sings. Such faith would have shot up in his heart, and have given him peace in thinking of his wife and little ones, had it not been disturbed by that homely remark of old Mr. Webster, "That God would n't undertake any work which the churches *shirked* off onto him."

24

But now his meditations were interrupted by Lucy's musical voice, carolling up stairs and down, as she flitted hither and thither, to find what was needed for packing the valise. It was not far from railroad time, — he too, must busy himself about the journey. He slipped his poor little 'will,' un-attested, into a drawer, and gave his attention to necessary work.

When he was fairly gone, Lucy sung no more, — for she was alone for the first time.

She took her child and sat with it by the parlor window, watching the passers by. There was a little yard belonging to "Number Five," in which Lucy had sowed grass. The snows had now melted, the south wind blew over it, the spring sun shone on it, and Lucy's pet grass already looked green. She held up her child to enjoy the sight with her, and as she did so, some one nodded. It was Marion Gray, one of the young ladies of their parish. In her hand she had a great doll which she held up, and this pleased the child more than the grass had done. Marion crossed over and came in, and gave the child the doll, for it had been purchased for that purpose, and she sat with Mrs. Holbrook until it grew late, and at length spent the night, and, after all, did not leave her until Mr. Holbrook's return. So Mrs. Holbrook was alone no more.

"I wonder," said she, in one of her daily letters to Mr. Holbrook, "how any one can get along without a *people*. I should feel lost; they seem to find ways of doing as much for us as we for them."

Mr. Holbrook, in reply, placed this passage side by side with one which Lucy had written before their marriage, when the prospect of being a city pastor's wife entirely overwhelmed her.

While Mr. Holbrook was absent, Mr. Sampson called.

"I'm glad he is gone," said he, when he heard of it, "he looked as if he needed rest. Between you and me, Mrs. Holbrook, my business this afternoon was to say to him, that I had been thinking lately he ought to have more books, and I should like to send part of my library to him. We folks who don't read much, an't so apt to remember that our minister, who lives by it, must have books."

"I am sure you are very kind, Mr. Sampson," said Lucy; "Mr. Holbrook does want more books than he can buy."

"I know that, and if I could have my way, I'd have our church own a minister's library, and place so much a year at his disposal to add to it and keep it in order. We have a fine place to keep one in our vestry; but I mustn't stop a

minute to talk about this; I can only say, that I
hope one of these days we shall bring it about.
I will send in the box some time towards night."

Mr. Sampson took his leave, and before night
his box came. Lucy unpacked it. It contained
a few standard religious works, Rise and Progress, Saints' Rest, Law's Serious Call, etc., —
but most of the books were odd volumes of tracts
and sermons, and religious periodicals. Lucy
looked about on the book-shelves, but she could
find no place where they seemed to belong, so
she put them in a corner to await the minister's
return; thinking he might value the feeling
which prompted the offering, more than the gift
itself.

Mr. Holbrook returned safely from his journey, much benefited. It seemed almost to have
made him over. He had eaten and slept, and
slept and eaten; his bronchial difficulties had
wholly disappeared, and he was ready to commence his work again with fresh zeal.

Lucy inquired if he had preached during his
absence; "yes, he had preached for Dr. Dodd,
and for another church which was then without a
pastor."

Lucy had not forgotten Dr. Dodd.

"Whereabouts did you find his church, — up
town?" she inquired.

"About half way up."

"He did not object to your preaching for him then?" said Lucy, with a sly look.

"No, so far from that he received me most cordially, and insisted upon my making my home at his house. He paid me every attention."

"I suspect you are getting to be more of a man than you once were," said Lucy, still laughing.

"Lucy, *we* certainly should be ready to make excuses for ministers. Since I have had a peep at his life, the thought has occurred to me, that he might have received courtesies from some of our city brethren, which he wished an opportunity to return. I was a stranger when I called upon him. I should like to have you see his wife, I know you would like her."

"I dare say," said Lucy, not yet sobered. "What did you preach?" Mr. Holbrook told her. "Why, those are the sermons which Herbert's father and Mrs. Foot thought so much of, though for the matter of that, they always like your preaching."

Mr. Holbrook now laughed heartily.

"Why, what is the matter?" said Lucy.

"They praise my sermons more than any two people in my church; and yet there are no two whose attention I find it so difficult to get."

"Does not Herbert's father listen? I thought he was one of your best hearers."

24*

"No; his eye wanders everywhere, and sometimes I cannot even keep him awake."

"It is just so with Mrs. Foot," said Lucy; "she nods every Sunday, and yet she thinks you have n't your equal in the city. We have to make great allowances both for their praise and their blame. How was it with Dr. Dodd's people, — were they interested?"

"They gave me good attention."

"And at the other church?"

"I never could ask for a more attentive audience than I found there."

CHAPTER XXX.

THE MOURNING MOTHER.

As the summer advanced, Lucy began to droop. The Downs Street people were scattering in search of cool breezes and pleasant shades. It seemed necessary that the minister and his family also, should go into the country for a season. To effect this, and yet not run in debt, required skilful and scientific manœuvres on Lucy's part.

The place chosen as their resort was near the city, and many strangers, even from a distance, were attracted there by its beauty. While there, Mr. and Mrs. Holbrook fell in with some members of Dr. Dodd's church; and from them, Lucy learned that Mr. Holbrook's preaching had excited much interest. The church without a pastor had been greatly captivated.

This information took Mr. Holbrook entirely by surprise. To be sure, when a student, he had dreamed of making some great impression by his preaching; but after he was settled and had entered upon his work, these dreams were lost in the earnestness with which he endeavored to discharge

faithfully, present duty ; or, if they ever occurred
to him, he felt the impossibility of their being
realized, while his great plans for study were
necessarily laid aside.   Could it be, after all, that
though forced out of paths of his own choosing,
he had been driven into others which were nearer
the goal?   It was even so.   His devotedness to
his work had led him to concentrate his strength,
and while seeking to teach, he had himself been
taught. From this chosen shelf of books, scarcely
had the dust been shaken, but that and the other
and the other had been thoroughly ransacked. In
one particular line, he had added nothing to his
store ; but in others, he had been amassing treasures, which, with his increasing discipline of mind
and vitality of heart, had already made him a pow-
erful and impressive preacher. Of all this, he was
unconscious.   He had been thus far absorbed by
his every day's work.   Thus the weaver plies his
busy shuttle to and fro, to and fro, — and by and
by the pattern, which a more skilful artizan than
he had planned, turns out complete.

These hopeful signs of progress and success,
aided by the genial influences of the country,
rapidly recruited the minister and his wife. They
returned in the autumn to " Number Five," ready
to recommence their work. The Downs Street
people also returned to their city homes, — and
life resumed its daily round.

Mr. Holbrook found so much to do immediately after his return, that his absent-mindedness increased upon him, and gave him much trouble. One instance of its effects he long remembered sadly.

Late in the season, he was returning with Lucy from Mr. Kennedy's, where they had been making a call. It was growing dark, and a lamp-lighter, with his blazing torch, was beginning his rounds. Lucy, in high spirits, was relating to him a recent adventure, when Mrs. Tileston, a young woman, met them. She paused to shake hands with her minister. Now it so happened, most unfortunately, that he had just received an important letter from Dr. Dodd, and his mind was wholly absorbed by its contents; he had indeed known but little of what Lucy had been saying to him.

"I hope you are all well at home," said he to Mrs. Tileston, making an effort to collect his thoughts; "and that fine little boy I baptized, — he grows, I hope."

O dear! O dear! for that poor broken-hearted mother. She gave him one look — so full of anguish, and then bursting into a flood of tears, she hurried past him. True — true, he had baptized that baby, — and he had also *buried* him.

"O, Charles!" said Lucy, "her baby is dead; did not you see that she was in deep black?"

"I had forgotten it," said he, stopping short, and looking after her. She was hastening on up the street, still weeping.

"I feel sorry for her," said Lucy; "she has never seemed like herself since the death of that child."

"How could I have forgotten it," said he, now walking slowly and sadly towards home.

How *could* he have forgotten it? — and yet it was not so very unaccountable. Death is a common event. The minister had buried many of his people since he laid that young mother's first-born in its little grave. Then, too, on that same day, a cherub boy had been born at "Number Five," and joy had driven grief from the father's mind. These circumstances, though they might excuse him, yet would not heal the wound which he had so unfortunately inflicted. He felt little appetite for his tea; he could not apply himself to his evening's work; that poor young mother's pale face haunted him, and he determined at length to go and see her at once, — and he did so. He found her sitting alone in her little parlor, idle and dejected, for what had she to work for now? Ah! it is night with us, when the angel of death comes, and bears away our little ones in his bosom. We cannot see the glory of his heaven-lighted path, or hear the music of his welcoming; for our eyes are blinded by tears, and our hearts are filled with sorrow. The cradle is empty, and the nursery is still, — and the night is very dark about us. So it was with this young mother. Mr. Holbrook sat down by her, and with much feeling explained to her the various circumstances which had for the moment driven her affliction from his mind. His sympathy was excited for her, — he wished much to comfort her; and his conversation and his prayer with her did comfort her.

"Beautiful are the feet of him who bringeth glad tidings," — who comes to us when we weep, *authorized* to say, "Sorrow endureth for a night, but *joy* cometh in the *morning.*" This is the privilege of him who is set apart to the work of the ministry.

As Mr. Holbrook returned to his home, he felt that such scenes were strongly attaching him to his profession and his people.

CHAPTER XXXI.

THE DOWNS STREET PEOPLE IN COMMOTION.

UNLOOKED for changes were awaiting the Downs Street minister. Before a tiny spear of grass was ready to show its green head in the little yard of " Number Five," Mr. Holbrook had received a unanimous call to settle over that vacant church in the city where he had preached when returning from his journey. A salary of three thousand dollars a year was offered him, with the additional inducement that his debts, if he had any, should be paid by his new friends, and, if he wished it, he should be released from his labors for a year, that he might travel in Europe. Letters from Dr. Dodd, and also from Dr. Barrows, urged him to accept the call.

Mr. Holbrook read these various letters, first at the post-office, and then hastened home; but, as Lucy was out, he shut himself into his study, and impatiently awaited her return.

When he heard her come in, he went to the stairs and called her. She came immediately.

"Has anything happened," said she, slightly alarmed by his excited manner.

"Yes," said he, holding out his hand to her, "come up, and I will tell you."

When Lucy heard the news, she was at first quite overcome. That Mr. Holbrook should have such a salary, — should have his debts paid, — should travel abroad when he so much needed it, — all this seemed too much to be true. She clapped her hands with delight. Already, in her imagination, were they beyond the necessity of economizing, — already were they rich and happy. These were her first gay thoughts, — her second thoughts were of a more serious character. The Downs Street people, their first love, began to gather about her, and "Number Five" seemed dearer than ever. There was the nursery, and here the pleasant green study, and yonder the familiar old church tower, with its friendly clock to keep the hours for them, and the sunset clouds behind it, blushing at the hour of evening; could she bid all these farewell?

"I should like to go," said she, giving utterance to both thoughts, "but I do not wish to leave here."

Mr. Holbrook had as yet no wish to express. The question for him to decide was one of life's great questions, and it required deliberate and

prayerful thought.   He wished to devote his time
entirely to it, and therefore requested his deacons
that evening, after lecture, to release him from the
charge of the pulpit for one or two Sabbaths, that
he might be at liberty to leave town if necessary.
While he was conversing with them, Lucy stood
waiting in the slip, watching the party.   A single
exclamation of surprise burst from the deacon when
Mr. Holbrook made his request, and then they
stood, with grave countenances, conversing.

"What is going on?" said Mrs. Kennedy, touch-
ing Lucy's shoulder.   "Our minister looks pale,
and the deacons are troubled.   Nothing wrong I
hope."

Lucy told her what was the subject of the conversation.

"He shall not go," said Mrs. Kennedy, "so
what is the use of talking about it.   If he goes,
we will go, church and all."

Her assertion did not seem to satisfy herself,
for she stood anxiously waiting as if impatient to
hear some result.

The party by and by walked slowly on.   Mrs.
Kennedy touched Mr. Holbrook.   "Surely you
won't *think* of going?" said she.   "A pretty piece
of work this, to come and get away our minister."

Mr. Holbrook had not considered the subject;
he had no opinion to give.

The news flew like wildfire among the Downs Street people, and they were in a great tumult. Bridget had as much as she could do to answer the door bell. Everybody was calling at "Number Five," to hear the truth for themselves.

There was old Mr. Webster, he was very restless; he would come twice a day. Mr. and Mrs. Roberts, Messrs. Mayhue and Sampson and Lovering, Mr. and Mrs. Vinton, Herbert's father and mother, deacon Silas, a few returned abolition friends, — and, many times, Mr. and Mrs. Kennedy came, as they said "they did not know what for, only because they could n't keep away. They could not spare their minister, and they must come and tell him so."

In the general overflow of feeling, presents came pouring in, as if all the days had been "donation days." Book-marks were left by scores, covered with the most affectionate inscriptions — "To their dear pastor," by the little ones in the flock. The Downs Street people seemed perfectly absorbed in their pastor, when they found themselves in danger of losing him.

In the midst of this enthusiasm, Lucy forgot all about her anxiety to be "out of debt and out of danger." Why should she care for three thousand a year? They had enough to get along with, prudently. Hearts such as the Downs Street people had, were not to be bought, — and thus she, also, became anxious to have the minister remain.

In the meantime he deliberated alone in his study. Why should he leave his people? Not for his salary, — not for the advantages of travel, — though these, to him, were no trifles, but should not he occupy a more important position than the one he at present held? Could he not make his influence more widely felt in the new field? This might be so, yet to him it seemed that much was due to his own church. He took a far-sighted view of their prospects; he, better than any one else, knew where the roots of their prosperity were silently spreading. Could a stranger develop them so well as he? Had not he and his people become of one heart and mind, and, if he should leave them just at this period of their history, would not his work for them be left unfinished? A few years more of prosperity, and his church could then, with comparative safety, be transferred into other hands; — that poor church, which had been roughly used by many a storm, and was now but just beginning to lift up its head. Should he leave it in its weakness, — perhaps for new storms to gather and break over it?

Another view, also, of the question before him, greatly interested his mind. Was it true that so much, as was often imagined in similar cases, depended on the 'position' of a pastor? Mr. Holbrook's 'position' as pastor of the Downs Street Church, had led him to reflect much on this; and it seemed to him that, after all, a man made his own position, — not the position the man. In his view of the providence of God, *that* seemed to honor 'character' more than 'circumstance,' — and might he not *trust*? Would not God use all his real character in that position to which God had first called him, and to which his youthful affections had been wedded?

These thoughts came silently in the study, and as yet no one knew of them out of it, so the people still called, anxiously inquiring.

One evening, Mrs. Tileston was announced. She brought with her a handsome cloak and cap which had been fitted for the lost one, and wished Lucy to make use of them for her own little boy. She also anxiously inquired, if any decision had yet been made. Lucy had heard of none. "I shall run in again to-morrow and ask," said she to Lucy. Just then Mr. Holbrook came into the entry. She immediately went to him, and taking his hand in both of hers said, with much feeling, "Mr. Holbrook, if they only knew *how much* we love you, they would not call you away."

"*I shall not leave you,*" was his reply.

CHAPTER XXXII.

"NUMBER FIVE" — IN THE DISTANCE.

IT is said that bad news travels post, while the good goes afoot. This certainly was not true in Mr. Holbrook's case; for within twenty-four hours, it seemed as if every member of his society knew that he was not to leave them. Mr. Holbrook quietly returned to his work, but not so his people. They were far from being quiet, — important projects were under consideration. Mr. Holbrook was soon informed that his salary was increased to two thousand dollars a year, and that a few of his more able friends stood ready to meet the expenses of his spending a year in Europe. It was evident to them that such a change would be beneficial to him, if indeed it were not an absolute necessity.

When the root of daffodil, which was the pride of Lucy's garden, showed its first white blossom, strangers alone looked upon it — for "Number Five" had been leased for a year. Mr. Holbrook was far away, and Lucy and her children were among the snows on the ' old farm.' Lucy had taken to her country home one little pet, — it was the poor woman's geranium. She one day, when turning its leaves to the sun, dropped silent tears on them, — she felt widowed. Before night her sadness all vanished, for she received a huge packet of letters from the absent minister.

" I am enjoying much," said he, in one of these; " a world of new thoughts are pouring in upon me. But I find myself often counting the days which must intervene before I shall be ' homeward bound.' I long to get back to my people. I feel an increasing sense of the importance of a *preacher's* work in this world. I reverence my *pulpit* more and more, and I thank God every day for having given me such a ' people ' to whom I may minister in his service. Nothing else makes long life so desirable to me, as the prospect of spending it just there where God has placed me, and amidst the ' chosen ones ' whom He has there gathered around me. By His grace, I mean to give myself to my work for them more devotedly than I have ever done before."

Such was the testimony of one respecting the ' Life of a City Pastor.' Lucy's was somewhat like it. Busy and toilsome as she had frequently found her life to be in the position of the city pastor's wife, she did not fully appreciate all its

privileges and enjoyments, until she left them for
a season. Then she missed her cares and labors,
her joys and sorrows for others, — for they had
kept every fibre of her heart warm and active ;
and that heart bounded at the thought of being
once more among the kind friends who used to be
running in and out, even in morning hours, just to
take a " Peep at Number Five."